Gor-geous…

Betsy closed her lips in an attempt to stifle the moan she felt building in her throat, a sound spurred on by the unexpected tingle that coursed through her body as the man stepped into the path of the sun, his sapphire-blue eyes dancing in its shimmering rays.

Her gaze slid down his face, taking note of everything from the chiseled jaw and kissable mouth to his uniformed broad shoulders and narrow waist. The effect his presence had on her was like nothing she'd ever felt before—startling, curious, undeniable.

And more than a little stupid. On so many levels.

She wasn't a hormone-crazed teenager. Not even close. She was a thirty-two-year-old widow with no interest in a relationship of any kind.

Second, there was no way the tingle in her body could be from him. She'd *just* laid eyes on him.

Third, and most important, he was a police officer—a fact that should have her running for the hills, not sitting there staring like a love-struck idiot…

Dear Reader,

Sometimes the turning point in a person's life comes from an unusual place—a book, a song, a dream. The key is *seeing* it....

And then doing something with it.

For my heroine, Betsy, the turning point comes from a picture on a bookstore calendar—a picture that propels her to travel nearly halfway across the country for a reason she can't explain to anyone, let alone herself.

But she takes a chance. On herself and her life. And as you'll soon see, it makes all the difference in her world.

I've been where Betsy was (but for different reasons), and I, too, was led toward change by the picture of a bridge.

A picture that now hangs on my bedroom wall.

Best wishes,

Laura Bradford

A Mom for Callie
LAURA BRADFORD

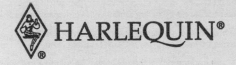

HARLEQUIN®

TORONTO • NEW YORK • LONDON
AMSTERDAM • PARIS • SYDNEY • HAMBURG
STOCKHOLM • ATHENS • TOKYO • MILAN • MADRID
PRAGUE • WARSAW • BUDAPEST • AUCKLAND

Recycling programs
for this product may
not exist in your area.

ISBN-13: 978-0-373-75319-2

A MOM FOR CALLIE

ABOUT THE AUTHOR

Since the age of ten, Laura Bradford hasn't wanted to do anything other than write—news articles, feature stories, business copy and whatever else she could come up with to pay the bills. But they were always diversions from the one thing she wanted to write most—fiction.

Today, with an Agatha Award nomination under her belt and a new mystery series with Berkley Prime Crime, Laura is thrilled to have crossed into the romance genre with her all-time favorite series, Harlequin American Romance.

When she's not writing, Laura enjoys reading, hiking, traveling and all things chocolate. She lives in New York with her two daughters. To contact her, visit her Web site, www.laurabradford.com.

Books by Laura Bradford

HARLEQUIN AMERICAN ROMANCE
1289—KAYLA'S DADDY

For my cop
From your writer

Chapter One

Betsy Anderson rested her chin on her knees as she studied the placement of each and every stone, her heart keenly aware of a budding feeling she'd nearly forgotten. A feeling she'd once thrived on, yet had learned to function without.

But even as she sat there in the grass, staring at the ornate yet simplistic structure and marveling at the emotions it evoked inside her, she knew how ridiculous her journey seemed. There were pedestrian bridges in New York City far more picturesque than the one in front of her. Still, something about *this* bridge had propelled her to toss what was left of her life into a suitcase and drive twelve hundred miles from home.

Just so she could see it.

It was ludicrous, really. Maybe even teetering on the edge of certifiable. But Paxton Bridge had stirred something inside her from the moment she saw its snowcapped image on the page of a bookstore calendar in midtown Manhattan. Its instantaneous grasp on her mind and heart had been completely unexpected, a sensation she'd been unable to explain to anyone, including herself.

At least that's what she'd told her neighbor as she

was packing her laptop and suitcase into the car, maps clutched in her free hand. She hadn't been intentionally evasive, she really hadn't. It was just something she couldn't put into words no matter how hard she tried.

Until now.

Now it was crystal clear. At least in her eyes. And probably to anyone who knew what it was like to lose sight of hope.

She exhaled a wisp of soft brown hair from her eyes and grinned as it fell back against her skin undaunted. It may have taken a while, a very long while for that matter, but for the first time in a year she finally felt as if things might get better. How, she didn't know quite yet. When, she wasn't exactly sure of, either. But deep down inside she finally knew it would.

And she owed it all to a stone bridge in the middle of a quaint little park in Cedar Creek, Illinois.

A low whistle cut through the silence of the warm April day and forced her gaze off the bridge for the first time in over an hour. The tune was familiar yet elusive, launching her into a visual game of hide-and-seek with a pair of navy blue legs she could see beneath the branches of an unending line of oak trees. Judging by their size and shape, they belonged to a male, his feet clad in black shoes, his gait one of confidence.

Curious, she leaned forward, watched as the accompanying hand reached down to retrieve a soda can off the ground and toss it into a nearby garbage can.

Considerate…

Her eyes tracked the legs as they continued on, their pace an interesting mixture of leisure and purpose. After several minutes they stopped once again, this time allowing the whistler to reach down and pat the head of a toddler riding by in a stroller with a tiny brown puppy in tow.

Sweet...

When the child grew bored, the legs moved on, prompting her gaze to follow suit. They reached a fork in the path and headed left, the color of the pants and the squeak of the shoes finally registering in some dusty corner of her mind.

Gor-geous...

She closed her lips in an attempt to stifle the moan she felt building in her throat, a sound spurred on by the unexpected tingle that coursed through her body as the whistler stepped into the path of the sun. Her gaze slid down from his face, taking note of everything from the chiseled jaw and kissable mouth to his uniformed broad shoulders and narrow waist. The effect his presence had on her was like nothing she'd ever felt before—startling, curious, undeniable.

And more than a little stupid. On so many levels.

First and foremost, she wasn't a hormone-crazed teenager. Not even close. She was a thirty-two-year-old widow with no interest in a relationship of any kind.

Second, there was no way the tingle in her body could be from him. She'd *just* laid eyes on him.

Third, and most important, he was a police officer—a fact that should have her running for the hills, not sitting there staring like a love-struck idiot....

Hadn't she learned *anything?* Hadn't one late-night knock at the door been enough?

"For a lifetime," she mumbled, her eyes widening as the words left her mouth.

Uh-oh.

But it was too late. The whistler paused midstride, his startlingly blue eyes now trained directly on her face.

"Ma'am?"

Instantly, the tingle-that-couldn't-have-been returned with a vengeance, this time with a slight moistening in her hands to boot.

"I, uh…" She looked around for something that would provide a graceful escape from the uncomfortable place she'd landed. "It's really quite beautiful," she said, gesturing toward the bridge out of desperation. "And more than a little inspiring."

She was grateful when his unreadable expression finally left her face and focused on the stone structure just over his right shoulder. It gave her a moment to breathe and regroup.

"The Paxton? Yeah, it's a gem. It took a lot of men a lot of blood, sweat and tears to build that bridge." He pulled his hat from his head and tucked it under his arm, his free hand gliding through his short dark brown hair with ease.

What would it feel like to run her hands through that hair?

"Ma'am, are you okay?"

Startled, she shook her head against the crazy images floating through her mind and forced herself to concentrate on the topic at hand.

"Do you know how long it took?"

"What? To make the bridge?" he asked.

She nodded.

"Almost twelve months to the day. My grandfather helped cart some of its stones back when he was a teenager. I think my mom still has a picture. She found it among his stuff after he died a few years ago."

She inhaled sharply, his words touching a place she knew all too well. "I'm so sorry. I didn't mean to stir up any bad memories."

The man shrugged, the buttons of his uniform rising up a hairbreadth before dipping back down. "Memories of my grandfather make me happy. And as for his death…well, he lived a good life, an honorable life. Can't ask for much more than that."

"Do you find yourself ever having any regrets when you think about him? Wait… You know what? Don't answer that. I'm just in a pensive mood, I guess." Pointing at the bridge, she quickly steered the conversation back on track. "It's about seventy-three years old, right?"

He looked at her, his lips closed together in a surprised smile. "Seventy-*four*, actually. But, I'm impressed. Seems most people around here don't think about it unless it's an anniversary year and the town throws a celebration bash." His gaze left her face long enough to study her immediate surroundings before reengaging eye contact. "We won't be having another one of those until late next year."

"A bash you'll undoubtedly miss on account of having to do crowd control, yes?"

He shrugged once again, his hands dropping to his hips as he widened his stance. "It's my job. Though the first two I worked were…hmm…*fairly* uneventful."

She laughed at the hesitation in his voice. "Fairly? Sounds like there's a story there."

"Several, actually." He pulled his hat from underneath his arm and fiddled with it between his hands, a telltale sparkle lighting his eyes. "You wouldn't believe what people do at those things…the trouble they can get themselves into without even trying."

"Try me." Stretching her jean-clad legs outward, Betsy winced at the soreness that came from sitting in the same position for entirely too long.

"You don't have work to do?" he asked as he gestured his head toward the notepad and pen she'd tossed onto her computer bag when she arrived.

She waved a dismissive hand in the air. "Oh, I've got work to do, all right. Over three hundred pages of work to do. Only I'm waiting until the elephant leaves the room."

"Elephant?" His eyes narrowed in intensity as he studied her once again. "I'm sorry, I'm not following."

"Right. How could you?" She swallowed back the wave of embarrassment that threatened to engulf her. "Sorry about that. Let's just chalk it up to the horrors of being another year older."

Seemed reasonable enough to her. And, come to think of it, maybe it even explained the recurring tingle in a roundabout sort of way. She said as much to the police officer. "Maybe instead of an overindulgence of sugar as is the norm on this day, maybe I'm babbling because I've not had enough."

"This day? I'm sorry but I'm still not follow—*wait!* It's your birthday?"

She nodded, her eyes meeting his as yet another tingle shot its way through her body.

"Well then, happy birthday. I hope it's a great day and an even better year."

"It can't get much worse." The second the words were out she regretted them, squirming at the bitterness in her voice. She really had become a wet blanket. A waterlogged wet blanket.

Leaping to her feet, she tugged the bottom of her baby-pink V-neck shirt down around her waist and forced a smile. "You know what? I'd like to scratch that comment from the record if we can. Birthdays are for fresh starts and new beginnings. And today's mine."

She tucked a strand of hair behind her ear, cocking her head slightly to the left as she took in the officer's perplexed—and more than a little amused—expression. "So, if it's all right, I'd like to respond to your statement once again."

Folding his arms across his chest, he flashed a smile that made her knees weak. "Okay..."

She felt her cheeks warm under his visual inspection as she shifted from foot to foot, waiting. "Please. Say it again. So I can respond more appropriately."

Understanding dawned in his sunlit eyes, a hearty laugh on its heels. "Oh. Right. My mistake." He cleared his throat and gestured in her direction. "I could make it sound even better if I knew your name."

"Betsy. Betsy Anderson."

His gaze roamed across her body as he nodded at the information, the naked appreciation in his eyes deepening the flush to her face. "Happy birthday, Betsy Anderson. I hope you have a great year."

Satisfied, she extended her hand in his direction, the feel of his skin imprinting on her memory. "Thank you, I hope so, too."

THERE WAS SOMETHING ABOUT Betsy Anderson that seemed to root his feet to the asphalt path and his gaze to her thickly lashed brown eyes. What exactly it was, though, he wasn't sure.

If it was even her at all.

Perhaps it was nothing more than the quiet day and the absence of activity in the park leaving him with little else to do. Perhaps it was the welcomed feel of the sun on his face after a long, miserable winter. Perhaps it was a stall tactic—a way to avoid headquarters and the chief's foul mood.

Or maybe it was the simple fact he hadn't been with a woman in more months than he could count and she brought the word *pretty* to a whole new level.

"You realize you know my name but I don't know yours, right?"

He was one of those guys who believed every woman had a feature that made her pretty—long legs, shapely curves, intriguing eyes, a cute nose... But Betsy Anderson had an *abundance* of pretty features, not the least of which was a smile that made him catch his breath every time it swept across her face....

"Okay, I'll guess. I'm a master at names. Jake? Robert? Steve?"

A smile he'd love to see as his hands glided around her back and pulled her against his—

"Joe? Sam? Oooh, I know—Thor?"

Thor?

He gave his head a good shake in an attempt to dislodge the parade of erotic images marching in front of his eyes. She was talking to him and he was standing there like a lust-struck idiot. "I'm sorry, I didn't—"

"You haven't heard a word I've said, have you?" she asked, her mouth curving into yet another smile that made his chest tighten. "I could kind of tell you were lost in thought."

If she only knew....

Then again, if she knew, she'd probably slap him. Hard.

Lowering his head, he simply nodded. "Guilty as charged."

"Is that your plea?" she teased, her smile touching off a sparkle in her eyes that rivaled the morning sun.

"Yes, ma'am."

"Okay…I'll let you off. *This* time." Her laughter, sweet and pure, filled the air around them, his body reacting to the sound in ways he hoped she didn't notice. "But next time you ask for someone's name you really should supply your own, as well."

"Oh. Yeah. Sorry about that." He swung his hat upward, adjusting it to sit squarely on his head. "I'm Officer Brennan. Kyle Brennan."

"Kyle," she repeated. "Kyle. That's not one I've used before. I like it."

"Used before?"

"I'm a wr—"

The crackle of his radio interrupted her words. "Post fifteen. Comm desk."

"Excuse me, I need to get this." His gaze flickered across Betsy's face, noted the way her lips pursed and her brows furrowed at the unwelcome distraction as he lifted the radio to his mouth and responded. "Post fifteen."

He didn't know why he should be surprised by the reaction. He'd seen it before. It was one of the main reasons he'd avoided anything resembling a relationship since Lila. Well, that and the thought of getting his heart ripped out for a second time.…

"Post fifteen, we've got a ten twenty-seven Romeo at Linton Bank and Trust. Two suspects. Both armed."

"Roger. Post fifteen responding." Kyle slipped the radio back into his belt as the call for backup continued, his heart pounding at the sudden change in his morning. For years Cedar Creek had been a quiet town—the kind of place where people went to bed at night with their front doors unlocked. But lately, things had changed. Robberies were springing up around town. First the hardware store, then the local mom-and-pop market. And now, the bank… It had to stop. "I gotta go. Have a great birthday."

And with that he was off, his feet pounding against the asphalt as he ran toward the park's border with Linton Street. When he reached the far side of Paxton Bridge, he glanced back over his shoulder for one last look at Betsy Anderson, a woman who'd managed to stir something inside him he'd thought was long gone.

Something that needed to *stay* gone…

For his sake. And for Callie's.

Chapter Two

The line was dwindling. Finally. As much as Betsy loved losing herself in her work, the dog-and-pony show that followed wasn't her cup of tea.

But neither was the idea of her books sitting untouched on a bookstore shelf. Or, even worse, being boxed up and returned to sender.

So she played along, attending signings and meet-and-greets at various stores around the country each year, a process she'd have been done with by now if she'd been working rather than traipsing halfway across the country in search of a bridge.

Today's signing was her penance, or, perhaps more accurately, her peace offering. A pathetic attempt at justifying a trip that had her editor seething and her agent sweating. Though, in all fairness, the seething and sweating had started long before her visit to Cedar Creek. She'd only made *that* decision forty-eight hours ago. Her inability to write had been going on for months.

Twelve to be exact.

She stared at a distant bookshelf, its neat row of colorful spines disappearing from view as she traveled a road she'd walked too many times during too many sleepless nights and too many unproductive days. A road littered with the kind of memories that had propelled her to drive twelve hundred miles in the hope she could finally lay them to rest. Once and for all.

And for a few moments it seemed as if it could happen—as if the prospect of forgiving herself and reclaiming her life was not only possible but within her grasp. Meeting Kyle Brennan, though, had ripped that away once again...

Officer Kyle Brennan.

For ten glorious minutes she'd felt alive in his presence, smiling and laughing for the first time in a long time. It was as if the glimmer of hope she'd found in the bridge had been igniting before her eyes—relaxing her enough to coax her soul out of hiding.

Until the call came, anyway. A call that had sent him off in a run and her heart into a panic...

"Ms. Anderson?"

The notion that he was running toward armed criminals had gnawed at her the rest of the morning, shrouding her in a funk of what-ifs and if-onlys. She'd never panicked when Mark had gone on a fire call. Never truly worried about his safety. He'd told her he could handle anything and she'd believed him like a naive idiot. Or, more aptly, like one half of a couple who'd stopped caring months befo—

"Ms. Anderson?"

A woman's voice filtered through her pity party, snapping her back to the here and now. Betsy looked up and offered what she hoped was a warm and welcoming smile despite the regret and worry that was weighing her down. "I'm sorry, I guess I zoned out there for a few minutes."

"It's okay." The woman inhaled sharply. "I know

you're done in about two minutes, but I purposely waited until the end so I could ask a few quick questions."

"As you can see—" Betsy pointed around the now-quiet nook the store staff had set aside for her appearance "—your timing paid off. You have my undivided attention. So how are you?"

"*Ecstatic.* I had no idea you were coming until I heard it through the grapevine at my gym this morning." The woman hugged the hardcover book tightly to her chest. "I think my squeal may have been responsible for one guy nearly choking himself on the bench press."

Her mouth slacked open. "Are you serious? Is he okay?"

The woman shrugged, her small turned-up nose flaring ever so slightly. "I imagine. I didn't hear otherwise. And I'm fairly certain Tom would have told me."

"Tom?"

"That's my husband. He's a police officer." The woman waved away her words like a swarm of pesky flies. "But enough about him. I've been a fan of your work from the moment *See Jane Land a Man* hit the shelves four years ago. It was hilarious and sad and amazing all at the same time."

"I'm glad you liked it." And she was. Appreciative readers made the public side of her job more bearable.

"Liked it? I loved it. And then, when *Excuse Me… Who Ordered Him?* came out, I loved that even more. Probably because that was about the time Tom had finally come to his senses and realized he had a good thing. A *damn* good thing."

Betsy laughed. "So you're happy then?"

The woman set Betsy's latest hardcover on the table. "I've never been happier. Though—" she looked from side to side and lowered her voice "—I don't like to tell him that too often in the interest of maintaining the upper hand. Keeps him on his toes, you know?"

She wished she did. But she really didn't. Whatever spark had drawn her and Mark together in the beginning had started to die out shortly thereafter.

Forcing her focus to remain on the present, she smiled up at the woman. "Shall I sign this to you?"

"Please! My name is Angela. Angela Murphy. Though just write 'Ang' if you would."

"Ang, it is." She lifted the silver pen and opened her most recent book to the title page, her hand gliding across it in flowery movements. When she was done, she closed the book and handed it back. "I hope you like it."

The woman laughed, a loud boisterous sound that turned more than a few sets of eyes in their direction. "I already read it. I came in and got it last fall when it first came out. But I've never had a signed copy of a book before so I decided to buy another one today. Tom will just have to deal with it."

She liked this woman. Liked her confidence and her easy laughter. "You could have brought in your copy, I'd have happily signed that for you."

Angela shook her head as she tightened her arms around her newly signed book. "So when's the next one coming out? Soon, right?"

"You sound like my agent. And my editor." Betsy looked down at the pen between her fingers and shrugged, the lightness of the past few minutes giving way to the heaviness of her heart once again. "I don't know. I wish I did, but I don't."

The woman's eyes widened in surprise. "I'm so sorry, I didn't mean to overstep. I know from your Web site that you've—" she stepped around the table and squatted beside Betsy's chair "—been through a lot this year and I imagine that makes it hard to write.

"Please know how sorry I am at your loss," Angela continued. "You've given so much to me the past few years."

"I've given you so much?" Betsy fiddled with the pen in the hopes of warding off the tears she felt forming behind her eyes.

"Your books—they bring me happiness. They make me laugh. They make me cry. And they teach me things about myself that I'm too busy to see sometimes. Tom likes them because—for the few hours it takes me to read each one—my mouth is actually silent."

"You said your husband is a police officer, right?" She stared up at Angela, the nagging question she'd carried around in her head for the past few hours needing an answer once and for all.

Angela nodded.

"Have you talked to him today?"

"I talk to him every day."

Betsy shook her head softly. "No, I mean, have you spoken to him in the last hour or so?"

The woman gave her a curious look. "I called him from the parking lot before I came in to see you."

"Is he...is he okay?"

"He's fine. He sounded adrenaline-ized but good."

"Adrenaline-ized?"

"Pumped up. He said they'd had an exciting day at the department and that he had lots to tell me when he got home."

Pumped up was a good sign. A very good sign....

A whoosh of pent-up air exhaled through her mouth as she opened her eyes and reached for Angela's hand. "Thank you."

A smile spread across the woman's face as she rose to her feet and leaned against a bookshelf. "I'm not sure why you're thanking me but you're welcome."

She wasn't really sure why, either. Other than the fact Angela's words had quieted the fear that had taken hold of her heart the moment Officer Brennan had run off. A fear she wanted to believe stemmed purely from a flashback and *not* from the undeniable attraction she'd felt to the man himself. "Can I ask you a question? A personal one?"

"Sure. Shoot."

She looked down at the pen, resisted the urge to play with it once again. "How do you do it? How do you watch your husband go off to work each morning and not worry about his safety?"

Angela shrugged. "Tom has wanted to be a police officer since he was two years old. Almost every photograph I've seen of him in his childhood has him wearing a police hat or a gun belt. It is, and will always be, his passion in life. Knowing that gives me comfort."

Comfort...

"He knows I love him. And even though it probably sounds corny...we truly are each other's better half. Do we argue? All the time. But even when we do, I know he loves me and he knows I love him. No silly disagreement over the remote control or the way my books seem to cover every inch of the house can or will change that. True love is true love. Knowing that gives me peace."

"True love is true love," Betsy repeated quietly. Perhaps that's why her heart hadn't been at peace in twelve months. Longer if she was honest with herself about the state of her marriage *before* the fire...

"I'm not sure I know what that feels like." She heard

the words as they left her mouth, felt the instant regret at sharing them aloud. In front of a fan, no less.

Angela offered a half smile, her gaze locked gently with Betsy's. "True love feels different...both physically and emotionally. When I met Tom, I had tingles every time I looked at him."

Tingles?

"My palms got all sweaty."

Sweaty palms?

"I thought about him all the time. I worried about him every time he went on a call."

"But I thought you said you *didn't* worry," Betsy interjected.

"Initially I did. And sure, sometimes I still do. But I know him better now. I know his work is important to him. That eases the worry most days. But if I didn't focus on that...then yeah...I could worry myself sick. The thought of never seeing Tom again, the though of never being held in his arms again, the thought of not being able to tell him I love him, the thought of not trying to turn him into a reader one day...it's unfathomable."

Betsy simply nodded. It was all so much to absorb. She'd never felt those things with Mark, not really, anyway. In fact, the only time she'd experienced tingles and sweaty palms and true worry was that very morning with—

"You've felt it before, haven't you?" Angela asked with a knowing rise of her eyebrow.

She shrugged. "I don't know. Can it happen in less than ten minutes?"

The woman's smile nearly cracked her face open. "It happened in *five* for me."

"Maybe for other people love happens like that. But for some of us I think it..." Her voice trailed off as her mind began picking apart her statement, dissecting and following it for plot potential as a familiar excitement bubbled up inside.

She finally had it. A story she could sink her teeth into. A story that would call on the experiences her editor was so gung ho on, yet grow forward in each subsequent page. A story about finding hope and learning how to live again.

Glancing at her watch, Betsy began stacking the fanned out bookmarks the store had placed on the edge of her signing table, her fingers anxious to return to her keyboard. "Angela, you have no idea how much you've helped me. When you asked about the next book, I didn't have an answer. Because, at that moment, there was no next book. But just as your true love happened in five minutes, I suddenly have a book I need to write. *Now.*"

"Seriously?" Angela gripped her book, her eyes sparkling as she watched Betsy gather her belongings. "Talking to me helped?"

"More than you can know." Stuffing her things into her tote, Betsy stood and hugged the woman as an indisputable reality grew in her mind.

For months she'd struggled to pull herself from the funk she'd been in since Mark's death. Yet, in less than a day of being in Cedar Creek, she'd experienced the first ray of hope she'd felt in a year *and* had the makings of another book growing in her mind. So why tempt fate by going back to New York prematurely?

The copper-haired woman squealed as Betsy stepped backward. "Can you give me a hint? You know…about the plot?"

"I can do even better. If you're willing…perhaps I

could pick your brain at various points throughout the book."

Angela's mouth dropped open yet no words came out.

"Maybe we could even meet over lunch." It was an offer she hadn't thought of initially, but now that she'd made it, she was glad. Angela was about her age, maybe a few years older. But she was a firecracker and Betsy needed a little spark in her life.

"But you live in New York."

"Not anymore. Not for the next few months, anyway."

"What are you saying?" Angela asked.

"I'm saying I'm going to write my book here... in Cedar Creek. I just need to find a small house to rent."

Angela grabbed Betsy's hand and squeezed it tightly. "Oooh, I know just the place. It's really cute—almost looks like a beach bungalow if you can picture something like that in the middle of Illinois. It'd be perfect for you. And it's in a really quiet neighborhood."

An undeniable surge of excitement coursed through her body as she realized what she was about to do. For the first time in a year she was finally moving forward. By her own doing. "Sounds perfect. Who should I call to take a look at it?"

"You're looking at her."

"You're a Realtor?" Betsy asked.

"No, but I know one and we can call him on the way. The house isn't far from here and it happens to be right next door to my husband's partner—who, by the way, is extremely cute."

"A police officer?" she repeated as her mind traveled back to Paxton Bridge and the memory of Officer Brennan running in the opposite direction.

"Uh-huh."

She shot her hand—palm outward—into the air and shook her head. "I'll have to take your word on his cuteness, Angela. I've got a book to write, remember? And besides, if and when I'm ready to date again, I think I'll stick to someone safer. Like maybe an accountant. Or a pharmacist." Betsy pushed a strand of hair from her eyes and flashed a grin at her new friend. "As for the rest, you really don't have to spend your afternoon touting me around. Your husband has stuff to tell you over dinner, remember?"

Angela laughed. "I remember. But he can wait. The faster we get you settled, the faster you'll finish your book. And trust me, Tom is supportive of anything that will give his ears a break for a few hours."

From a purely aesthetic standpoint, Tom Murphy was nothing to envy. His hair, which had begun receding when he was a recruit, was now nonexistent. His short stature, set off by a tendency to gain weight at the drop of a hat, resembled that of a bulldog. And his inability to tuck in a shirt or polish his shoes had been a thorn in the chief's side for as long as Kyle Brennan could remember.

But it was Tom.

And after five years of working side by side, Kyle knew better than anyone what the disheveled package held inside. It was why, even as he listened to his partner talking animatedly into his cell phone, he couldn't begrudge him the happiness he'd found.

Begrudge? No.

Envy to the point of jealousy? Yeah, sometimes.

It was a fact he wasn't proud of, but it was what it was. Tom had been blessed to find a true one-in-a-million in Angela. Kyle, on the other hand, had quite obviously found Lila in the dime-a-dozen camp—a group of women who were entirely too self-absorbed to think of anyone else's needs, least of all their own child.

Hindsight sucked. It really did. Because it came too late. Too late to save him from the anger, disillusionment and wariness that had settled around his heart like a comfortable and well-worn blanket.

Then again, if it hadn't been for Lila, he wouldn't have Callie. And Callie made every kick in the gut from her mother worth it a million times over.

"Man, is Ang pumped right now." Tom snapped his cell phone closed and tossed it into the empty cup holder between their seats as he made a right onto West Fall Avenue and an immediate left onto Creek Bed Drive. "Not only did she get to meet this hotshot writer but they hit it off. They've apparently spent the past hour hanging out together and now we're taking her out for pizza tonight to celebrate her birthday."

Kyle pulled his gaze from a group of little boys playing kickball in a side yard and peered at his friend. "You lost me. What hotshot writer?"

"Elizabeth Lynn Anderson. Ang has read every one of her books." Tom yanked the car to the right to allow a delivery truck to pass on the narrow road flanked by parked cars. "Every time she reads one she gets all emotional. You know, giggly…weepy…horny."

He raised an eyebrow at his partner. "Horny?"

"Oh, yeah."

"If reading this chick's books gets Ang horny, what's meeting her going to do?"

"I don't know, man, but I can't wait to find out."
Rising up off the seat, Tom peeked into the rearview
mirror, a mischievous smile spreading across his face.
"Seriously, wouldn't this mug make *you* horny?"

"Truth?" Kyle shook his head as his laugh echoed
through the car, a sound he rarely made unless he was
with Tom or Callie. "Hey, I really appreciate you giving
me a lift today. Callie had a scout meeting after school
today and my mom's car is on the fritz."

"No prob, you know that. Besides, it just builds Ang's
anticipation," Tom replied with a self-satisfied smirk.

"So, this writer is famous?" Kyle shifted in the passenger seat in an effort to stretch his legs as far as possible despite the cramped quarters of a car made for a
short man like Tom. "What's she doing in Cedar Creek
of all places? Shouldn't she be holding court in more
worthwhile locales like New York or L.A.?"

"More worthwhile locales? C'mon, man, you don't
mean that…right?"

He shrugged and looked out the window at the passing homes and well-kept yards of the blue-collar town
he'd called home all his life, a town that hadn't been
big enough to keep Lila happy. "For someone like this
Elizabeth person, yeah I mean it."

"You don't even know her, Jerk Face." Tom switched
off the radio, silencing the music Kyle hadn't even realized was playing. "I mean, c'mon, you know Ang. She
can be tough on people. But you should have heard her
just now…she wouldn't sound like that if this woman
was like…" His partner's voice trailed off momentarily
only to return just as clear without so much as a hint of
reservation. "Lila."

He shrugged again, this time following up the sullen

gesture with a swift hand through his hair. "Even Ang can be wrong."

For several long minutes neither man said a word as Kyle pressed his forehead against the side window and closed his eyes. He was tired, that was all. He'd been on his feet all day, patrolling the park and chasing down the robbery suspects. Tiredness spawned grumpiness, didn't it?

"Do you hear how bitter you've gotten?" Tom's words, firm and strong, snapped him back to the moment. "I know Lila hurt you, Ky, but c'mon that was over six years ago. Let. It. Go."

"Let it go?" he snarled. "Let it go?"

"Yeah. Let it go. I get that she hurt you. I get that raising Callie alone is tough. But none of that should be hoisted onto a woman you don't even know. *That* is bitter. And unfair."

He opened his mouth to fight back then shut it without uttering a single word. Was Tom right? Was he really bitter?

"Maybe if you'd just get out there again…find a nice woman instead of just an occasional one-nighter. I mean, c'mon, man, my life is a million times better with Ang in it."

"Ang is different. She gets your passion for the job… she's loyal, she's grounded and she's real." And she was. He just needed someone softer. More vulnerable. Funny. Sweet. Pretty…

Like the woman in the park.

Betsy?

He bolted upright in his seat.

"Something wrong?" Tom cast a glance in his direction, a strange look playing behind his eyes. "You look like you just got slapped upside the head."

Should he tell him? And if he did, what would he say? There really wasn't anything to tell. Other than he'd struck up a conversation with a beautiful woman in the park that morning—a woman who seemed both vulnerable and strong all at the same time. A woman who made him laugh. And flirt. And think dirty thoughts.

Until he'd been raised by dispatch and her whole demeanor had changed…

Nah, there wasn't anything to tell. The last thing he needed was to put his heart on the line again.

To Tom, he just shook his head. "I'm okay. Just tired. Maybe a little cranky. That perp from the bank had a real mouth on him." He raked his hand through his hair as he continued. "And did you see the way he looked right at the news camera when I carted him out to the car? Most perps shield their eyes, but this guy? He seemed to *want* the glare."

"His one and only fifteen minutes of fame, I guess."

He groaned away his pent-up frustration. "What is it about fame that makes people take leave of their senses? Walk away from their own kid?" He turned and stared out the window.

"Not everyone is like Lila, dude."

"Whatever," he mumbled under his breath as his partner made the final turn onto Picket Lane. He knew he was being a downer but he couldn't stop. How was it that a day could start so well, so full of promise, and then suddenly take a nosedive?

"Hey…do me a favor, will you?" Tom pulled the car to a stop across from the pale yellow one-story home where Kyle lived with his seven-year-old daughter. "Slap a muzzle on the bitterness long enough to be polite, will you? Do it for Ang if not yourself."

"What are you talking about?" Kyle's gaze followed the path his partner's index finger made in the direction of the vacant home next door to his own.

"The author. She's looking at the Rileys' place."

"Author?"

"Yeah. The one I just told you about, idiot." Tom looked out the window once again, his finger finding his target. *"Her."*

Kyle stared out the window at Tom's wife and the petite brunette with the hot little figure standing in front of the Rileys' house.

"Betsy?" he whispered.

"You know her?" Tom asked.

"Well, sort of…a little, I guess. But her name's Betsy Anderson…not Elizabeth Lynn whatever you said."

"Anderson."

"Yeah. Ander…" He looked from the brunette to his partner and back again, reality dawning like a slap across the face. "Aw man, I sure can pick 'em, can't I?"

Chapter Three

"So, do you like it? I mean *really* like it?" Angela took Betsy's arm as they stepped off the small porch and headed down the front walkway. "It's in really good shape and I can virtually guarantee Jack Riley will be a wonderful landlord."

"I love it. It's perfect." She did and it was. In fact, Betsy couldn't have dreamed up a better hideaway if she tried. "That little sunroom off the back of the house will be perfect for writing. And the price is phenomenal."

Angela clapped her hands together and squealed. "I can't believe you're really going to write your next book right here in Cedar Creek!"

"And picking your brain as I go," Betsy reminded her with a smile.

"Trust me, I haven't forgotten that part. Though I'm afraid I'm going to wake up in the morning and find out this was all one big crazy dream."

As they stepped onto the sidewalk that ran along the eastern edge of Picket Lane, Betsy stopped and turned back toward the house, the crisp navy shutters popping against the khaki-colored siding. It was hard to believe she had a home, a real home. Sure she liked her tenth-story apartment off West Sixty-seventh in Manhattan.

But that was an apartment—a typical dinky overpriced New York City apartment. *This* was a home. A real home with a yard and trees…

Her home. For the next few months, anyway.

"If you find out it is a dream, don't tell me. Okay?"

"Deal." Angela pointed to the pale yellow house next door, a home with a similar look and feel as Betsy's rental. "You couldn't ask for a better neighbor than Kyle Brennan. Having a cop next door is like having a built-in security system without the monthly fees."

"Did you say Kyle Brennan? *Officer* Kyle Brennan?" She knew she must look like an idiot, standing there staring at this woman with her mouth nearly touching the concrete, but—

"Ang!"

They both turned toward a short squatty guy with a bald head and mismatched clothes headed in their direction, Kyle Brennan a few giant steps behind. Betsy felt her mouth go dry with relief.

"You're okay," she whispered as the man who'd plagued her thoughts all afternoon stepped closer, the late-afternoon sun dancing across his dark brown hair and sending her pulse racing.

Cocking his head a hairbreadth to the side, Kyle Brennan studied her face—a visual inspection she didn't mind in the slightest. "Of course I'm okay…why wouldn't I be?"

"Tom, I want you to meet Elizabeth Lynn Anderson. The woman who was responsible—in part—for me giving you the time of day way back when." Angela shot a pot-stirring smile in her husband's direction followed by a playful wink. "And, Elizabeth, this is Tom. My personal stud."

Grateful for the distraction, Betsy laughed and

extended her hand, a peaceful warmth settling over her topsy-turvy heart as Angela's husband engulfed it inside his own.

"It's an honor to meet the woman who can leave my wife speechless for an extended period of time." Tom Murphy released her and wrapped a loving and protective arm around the spitfire beside him. "You'll have to excuse the way I look right now. I dropped off my uniform to get pressed and—"

Angela coughed. "Don't listen to him, he always looks like that. In fact, the only time he matches is when he's in uniform."

Planting an amused kiss on his wife's head, Tom reclaimed the conversation. "So, Elizabeth, my Ang tells me you're planning on staying in Cedar Creek?"

"Betsy, please. Elizabeth is my pen name. Betsy is me…the real me." She allowed her gaze to move from Angela, to Tom, and back again before finally coming to rest on Kyle Brennan. "I've decided to get out of a horrible rut I've been in lately and Cedar Creek seems like the perfect place to start—"

"Daddy! Daddy! You're home!" A little girl with strawberry-blond hair and a brown beret and matching vest came hurtling down the driveway beside Kyle's home, her tiny feet pounding against the concrete as she ran in their direction and launched herself into Officer Brennan's arms. "I get to sell cookies this year, Daddy!"

"You do? Well, sign me up. I'll take one of everything." Betsy watched in awed surprise as the object of her revived tingling spun the little girl around before gently setting her down on the pavement and tousling her hair with his strong—and ringless—left hand.

The little girl giggled, dimples carving holes into her

round cheeks as her sapphire eyes—a perfect replica of her father's—twinkled in the sun's lingering rays. "Even the one with nuts? You hate nuts, Daddy."

Scrunching his face, Kyle rubbed his chin with one hand and scratched his head with the other. "Hmm. You're right. Maybe I'll take two of everything...*except* for the one with nuts."

"And we'll take two of those." Angela bent down and gave the little girl a big hug, releasing her long enough to fix the curled hair Kyle had tousled. "I love nuts."

"Nuts it is. And how about you? Would you like some cookies, too?" Kyle's daughter reached a tiny hand in Betsy's direction and flashed a shy yet friendly smile. "We got to try chocolate peanut butter ones at our meeting today and they were the yummiest cookies I've ever had. Well...'cept maybe the really, really yummy chocolate chip ones I make with Grandma."

"Callie, it's not polite to ask people to buy things when they don't even know you. Let's save cookie-selling for Grandma and my friends at the department."

The little girl's eyes dropped, her smile slipping from her face. "I'm sorry. I—"

Bending at the waist, Betsy nudged Callie's chin upward until their gazes were locked once again. "I'd be happy to buy cookies from you. With a recommendation like the one you just gave, I'd like two boxes of the ones you tried at your meeting." As the child's mouth turned upward once again, Betsy gave her small nose a gentle tap. "I love cookies when I'm writing. They help me think."

"Writing?" Callie's eyes grew wide as the dimples returned. "Do you write poems, too?"

"Ms. Anderson writes stories for big people like

me," Angela said in between daggered looks in Kyle's direction. "And she is very, very good at it."

"Do you write poetry, Callie?" Betsy reached out to tuck an errant strand of hair behind the child's ear but stopped as she felt Kyle's penetrating gaze.

"I do. All the time. Miss Lionetti even used one on the front page of the school's Christmas book this year."

"Wow. That's mighty special. I didn't get published until I was twenty-eight and you're what…seven?"

The child beamed proudly. "How'd you guess?"

Betsy shrugged. "I don't know. You just look like you're seven."

"Wow. A real book writer! Wait till I tell the kids at school tomorrow." Callie wrapped her arms around Betsy's neck and gave a quick squeeze. "I'm gonna go tell Grandma 'bout you." She turned toward her home and then stopped, her eyebrows furrowed together as she addressed Betsy once more. "How will I get your cookies to you when they come in?"

Betsy straightened up and waved her hand in the direction of the house next door. *Her* house. "Just knock on my door."

The little girl's mouth widened into a near perfect O as Betsy's words hit home. "You mean, you live there?"

"As of tomorrow, yes."

"Wow! Cool!" Callie took off in a run only to stop once again, her sweet voice carrying across the freshly manicured lawn and single-car driveway that separated the two homes. "Could I show you some of my poems one day?"

"Callie, that's enough. Go on inside and I'll be there in a minute." Kyle folded his arms across his chest, his mouth set in a tight line. To Betsy he said, "You don't have to—"

"I'd love to, Callie," she answered, her words successfully cutting off her next-door neighbor's surprising stiffness.

As the child made her way into the house after one final wave over her shoulder, Tom shook his head, a hearty laugh escaping from somewhere deep inside his soul. "That one's a pistol, ain't she? Cute as a button."

"She sure is," Betsy whispered as she waved once again to the little face now peering out from a curtained front window with a gray-haired woman standing beside her small form. "Absolutely precious."

After several long moments, Kyle broke the silence between them, his voice clipped and businesslike. "It seems to me that a place like Cedar Creek might be too small for a person with a pen name. There's really nothing special about this town. Nothing that can compare with L.A. or New York or wherever it is you're from."

"Kyle!" Angela snapped. "What on earth is wrong with you?"

Betsy slowly raised her palms into the air as Tom shook his head and looked skyward, muttering something under his breath about bitterness.

"It's okay, Angela. I'll take this." She wasn't sure how or why, but it was obvious that she'd rubbed Kyle Brennan the wrong way. And, truth be told, he was starting to do the same with her. The man standing in front of her now was a far cry from the fun-loving guy who'd wished her a happy birthday beside Paxton Bridge that very morning. That guy she liked, lusted even. This guy, though, was unfriendly and rude at best.

Carefully, she chose her words—words that would sum up how she felt without begging this man for something she didn't need from him, tingles be damned. "I'm from New York. The Upper West Side to be exact. But just because I love the excitement of the city doesn't mean I'm immune to the charms of a small town or—" she glanced at Angela and grinned "—its amazing people. As for whether Cedar Creek is too small for a person with a pen name…I suppose you're right…for *some* people. But writing is what I *do*. It's not who I *am*. Whether you choose to believe that or not is entirely up to you, Officer Brennan."

SHE COULDN'T HELP IT. She envied the genuine affection Angela shared with her husband. It was fun, spontaneous, real and like nothing she'd ever experienced in her lifetime. And the way he *looked* at her….

Betsy pulled her gaze from the couple seated on the opposite side of the table and lowered it to the menu in front of her, grateful for the chance to collect her thoughts after a day of highs and lows. In the time span of just a few short hours she'd taken more positive steps forward than she had in months, yet for some reason she'd allowed Tom's partner to cast a cloud over everything with his rude behavior.

How could someone be so kind and so friendly one minute only to become ill-mannered and standoffish the next?

"Betsy?"

Seriously, it was as if the Kyle Brennan she met alongside Paxton Bridge that morning was a different person from the man she met outside her new home.

"Earth to Betsy…"

Tom's voice filtered through her ears, interrupting her thoughts. "I'm sorry, did you say something?"

"I was trying to but you were a million miles away." Tom took a quick pull of his beer. "You okay?"

She forced the corners of her mouth upward in what she hoped was a real smile. It wasn't their fault that their friend was such an idiot. "Sure. Just thinking about the house, I guess."

"You mean, your rude neighbor," Angela interjected as she leaned her head against the cushioned seat back. "I had a good mind to slap him. Hard."

"Yeah, I'm sorry about that, Betsy. Kyle's not normally quite so...so—"

"Rude? Inconsiderate? Jerkish?"

Tom gestured toward his wife and nodded. "Yeah... what my wife just said. But seriously, he's not normally like that."

"He's not?"

"Aw, c'mon now, Ang. He's a total wuss where Callie is concerned, you know that."

Angela cocked her head to the side and nodded at Betsy. "That's true. Callie Brennan has her father wound around her finger tighter than any child I've ever seen... and he loves every minute of it."

Pushing the menu to the side, Betsy planted her elbows on the edge of the table and dropped her chin into her hands. "I could see that. His face lit up the moment she started running down the driveway. It's just a shame he couldn't hold it in place while he met his new neighbor."

"It's not you. Not you-you, anyway." Tom took another pull of his drink then wiped his mouth with the back of his hand. "He's got a thing with...well...fame, I guess."

"I don't follow," she said, her curiosity aroused despite the voice in her head that was trying to convince her it didn't matter—that *Kyle Brennan* didn't matter.

"Kyle's ex-wife was an actress," Angela said as she picked up the story from her husband. "They met when she was doing local theater one town over. She craved fame. Absolutely loved the spotlight…made sure her hair was perfect 24/7…never left home without her makeup flawless."

"O-kay…" Betsy prompted as she waited for the part that could even come close to explaining the man's behavior.

Angela pushed her hand through her hair and then leaned into the crook of her husband's arm. "Anyway, when she became pregnant with Callie, she wasn't exactly thrilled. She despised the weight she gained and absolutely hated the sleep-deprived circles under her eyes after the baby was born."

Betsy inhaled sharply as Angela continued, her heart bracing for the path she knew the story was about to take.

"Throw in the fact that Kyle was working swing shifts and hardly ever home, and, well, the novelty of parenting—if there ever had been a novelty for Lila—wore off inside six months. One day she simply packed her bags, left divorce papers on the kitchen table and headed for Hollywood. She hasn't looked back since."

Stunned, she looked from Angela to Tom and back again as her mind replayed everything she'd just heard. "How could…how could—" she shifted in her seat "—I mean, what about Callie? Does she at least keep in touch with her?"

"Lila refers to her as her niece whenever she's interviewed by the press these days." Tom chugged the rest of his beer then set the empty bottle at the end of the table. "Not that any of this is meant to be an excuse for his rudeness, because it's not. It's just…I don't know… an explanation, I guess. He really is a good guy."

She considered Tom's words, realized they made sense of the extremes she'd seen in Kyle. When they'd first met, she was simply Betsy—a woman sitting in the park. But later on, outside his home, she was Elizabeth—a well-known author. Her fame, or what he perceived as her fame, had stirred up emotions in Kyle she was just now beginning to understand.

"So what do you say, ladies? What looks good to you?" Tom motioned toward the menu. "I'm starving."

Forcing her attention to the couple across from her, she shrugged. "I'm easy."

Angela gasped. "Don't say that! We'll end up with a pizza covered in stuff that was never meant for human consumption. Besides, it's your birthday…so it's your choice."

She pulled her cast-off menu into view once again, her finger slowly moving down the list of choices. The appetite she'd had when they walked into the restaurant had all but disappeared, her stomach queasy from tales of Kyle's atrocious ex-wife.

"I don't know." She looked up at Tom, guilt making her head tilt. "I hate to say it but I tend to lean toward boring."

Angela clapped her hands together as a squeal erupted from her lips. "Ooh, I knew I liked you, Betsy."

Rolling his eyes toward the ceiling, Tom shook his head. "Don't tell me…you're a plain-cheese girl, too?"

She nodded sheepishly.

"No black olives…no 'shrooms…no buffalo chicken… no—"

"Don't you know it's not polite to coerce the birthday girl, Tom?"

Startled, Betsy looked up, her mouth gaping open at the sight of Kyle standing beside their table, his white button-down shirt pulled taut across his muscular arms and chest, his sapphire blue eyes trained on her face. Before she could formulate a response, he dropped his keys onto the table and gestured toward the empty spot on her side of the booth. "Any chance there's room for one more?"

HE SLID ONTO THE VINYL BENCH beside Betsy, his mind keenly aware of the thumping inside his chest that started the moment he spotted her across the restaurant. Sure, maybe some of it was simply discomfort at the notion he'd acted like a real jerk back at his place. And maybe some of it was the probing questions he knew he'd be subjected to at the station house the next morning when Tom and he were finally alone. But those things were a better explanation for the fleeting uncertainty he'd felt while crossing the room unnoticed. The thumping in his chest was all Betsy...

And the seemingly innocent black T-shirt that hugged her chest in a most provocative manner.

"Weren't you wearing a pink shirt this morning?"

Her brows furrowed as she considered his question. "I—I guess."

"And an off-white sweater set when you were outside my house?"

Tom snorted back a laugh. "Looking to emulate her wardrobe there, buddy? Because, really, of the two...I'm not sure off-white is your color."

Kyle groaned, his gaze locking with Angela's across the table. "How do you put up with this guy?"

"He's really good in bed."

Puffing his chest outward, Tom shifted in his seat, his ensuing smile threatening to crack his face in two. "And, Ky, my man…feel free to repeat my wife's words during roll call in the morning—"

"You never said it was going to be filtered through the department, baby. You just said you'd give me twenty bucks if I actually said—" Angela's voice disappeared behind Tom's pudgy hand as Betsy's laugh mingled with Kyle's.

There was no doubt about it, Tom and Angela were the quintessential perfect match right down to the good-natured teasing that made them slip into their own little world from time to time. Seizing the opportunity his friends' playful bantering provided, Kyle turned his attention back on Betsy, her smile tugging at his heart in the same way it had that morning beside Paxton Bridge.

"Look, I'm really sorry about my attitude earlier. I think the day just got the best of me and I took my crankiness out on you. I'm sorry."

He couldn't tell if she'd accepted his explanation, but he was grateful for her willingness to let bygones be bygones as her shoulders relaxed and conversation flowed between them. Once the agreed-upon pizza was ordered, talk volleyed around the table on everything from books to music to crazy high school memories… all harmless topics that steered them away from the one issue he wanted to avoid lest his bitterness rear its head once again. But by the time the pizza and drinks had been consumed, Kyle realized it didn't matter what the woman sitting beside him did for a living. All that mattered was the simple fact that she was breathtakingly beautiful, full of fun, genuinely sweet and an amazing listener.

Maybe Tom was right. Maybe Lila was a fluke....

"Woo-ee, how are you able to work beside such a good-lookin' dude like myself each and every day and not develop an inferiority complex?"

Tom's words wrestled Kyle's attention from Betsy. "What on earth are you blabbering about now?"

"Over there." His partner's hand rose into the air, his index finger directing everyone's eyes to the ceiling-mounted television screen in the back of the pizza joint. "But be honest...does the camera make me look fat?"

Kyle's laugh died on his lips as he focused on the screen, the on-air reporter standing in front of a now dark Linton Bank and Trust. As he watched, the camera cut—once again—to footage shot earlier as members of the Cedar Creek Police Department milled around outside the bank following that morning's robbery. Seconds later, Kyle, himself, appeared on the screen as he handcuffed one of the suspects and led him to an awaiting patrol car.

"Man, you were right...look at the way he's staring into the lens, looking for his moment of fame."

Kyle nodded, his attention still on the screen.

"I don't know, baby, that doesn't look like a guy mugging for the camera to me."

"You don't think so?" Tom asked.

"No. He looks—"

"Angry," Kyle finished for Angela as the report ended and he turned back to his partner. "Furious, even."

"If you ask me, it almost seemed as if he was looking into the eyes of someone he knew." Betsy's voice, soft and clear, drew him up short.

He stared at her. "What do you mean?"

"I don't know, it just seemed like his expression…his eyes…were saying something." Betsy dropped a piece of pizza crust onto her plate and pushed it to the side as her cheeks tinged red. "I'm sorry, don't mind me. I tend to look for a story everywhere. It's a pitfall of being a writer, I suppose. My mind rarely shuts off."

"Then you're in good company, Betsy. A cop's mind doesn't turn off, either," Tom said as he lifted his second empty beer bottle into the air in a mimed toast.

"It looks pretty turned off to me when you're asleep on the recliner with drool pooling in the corner of your mouth," Angela quipped as she pressed a playful elbow into her husband's side.

"Hmm. Now that sounds enticing after the day we had." Planting yet another kiss on his wife's head, Tom nodded across the table at Kyle and Betsy. "Any chance we could pick this up another day? With maybe a few more toppings next time?"

Again Angela poked him.

"What? I'm tired."

Betsy's sweet laugh filled the air, filtering its way into his memory bank along with the scent of lilacs that clung to her hair. "That was quick."

"Everything, and I mean, *everything,* with Tom is quick." Angela lifted her purse from the bench seat and smiled at Betsy across the table. "I can't even begin to tell you how incredible today was. I'm honored to have been able to spend your birthday dinner with you."

Kyle took in Betsy's flushed cheeks as she offered her own round of thanks in return. Her response, her gestures, her mannerisms were so unlike his ex-wife who had treasured the adoration of fans as much as she did her time in the spotlight. If anything, it seemed as if

Betsy Anderson was almost uncomfortable in whatever amount of celebrity skin she wore.

"Wait! Your car is back at the bookstore." Angela stopped midscoot and looked from Tom to Betsy and back again. "I completely forgot."

"I'll get her to her car. You two go on home."

Angela's eyebrow arched. "Will you be nice?"

He felt his face warm as he peeked at Betsy beside him. "Of course."

"Because you weren't earlier." Ang folded her arms across her chest and narrowed her gaze at Kyle as she waited for a response.

"I know." It was all he could think to say. Telling his partner and his partner's wife that he wanted them to leave was out of the question. Though, if Angela persisted, he might have to go that route. Anything to score a little time alone with Betsy.

Betsy.

Shifting his attention to the woman seated next to him, he offered what he hoped was a nonthreatening smile. "Is that okay with you? If I drive you back to your car?"

Her smile was all the answer he needed.

When Angela and Tom had gone, he studied her closely. "I just realized something."

"What's that?" she asked as their eyes met.

"You didn't have a cake."

Her hand, slender and petite, cut through the air, grazing his shoulder in the process. "This dinner was enough. Truly. It was fun. And that's something I needed far more than a piece of cake."

"You sure?"

She nodded, her hair falling forward across her forehead. "I'm sure."

Grabbing hold of the check he'd eyed Tom into leaving, he motioned toward the door, his heart rate increasing at the notion of being alone in a car with Betsy. "Shall we?"

THEY CHATTED AS HE DROVE, her curiosity about the shops and local landmarks they passed endearing her to him all the more. If he were honest with himself, Lila had never had any interest in Cedar Creek. Except maybe for which cross-country bus line it was on. Betsy, on the other hand, seemed to be genuinely interested in his hometown, asking questions and listening to his answers with rapt interest.

"When I first came here, I wasn't sure I could explain why. I mean, I left my apartment, jumped in my car and drove all night to see some bridge that caught my eye from the pages of a calendar." The sound of her sweet laughter made him listen even closer. "At first I thought it was about hope. And I still do. But I also think it symbolized a kind of peace that I need more than I ever realized."

He glanced over at her, her words taking him by surprise. "I wouldn't think a place like this would hold much interest for someone who is used to the hustle and bustle."

"Sometimes hustle and bustle makes you miss the little things. The things that matter most." Betsy pointed at the lone car in the bookstore parking lot. "That's my car right there."

Nodding, he pulled alongside her car and shifted his own into Park, his reluctance over the end to their evening impossible to ignore. Whatever it was about Betsy

Anderson that had stirred some long dormant excitement in his soul that morning had resurfaced in spades.

"I had a really nice time tonight. And your daughter is precious."

He nodded again, his gaze locked on hers. "So did I. And thank you—she's the light of my life."

"I can see why."

"You should have heard her this evening before I left for the restaurant. She's all excited at the notion of living next to an author." He swiveled to the side and draped his arm casually over the back of Betsy's seat. "In fact, when I left, she was making a birthday card for you at the kitchen table."

"A birthday card? How did she know?"

"I guess I mentioned it."

Her laugh echoed inside the closed car as she leaned against the seat, the tease of her hair against his hand sending a pulse of desire through his body.

"You know what?" she asked. "I can't remember the last birthday I enjoyed as much as this one."

"Even without a cake?"

"A cake with candles isn't what makes a birthday special. Smiles and laughter—the kind that make you feel whole—does. And therefore I couldn't have asked for a better birthday."

He studied her animated face in the glow of a nearby streetlamp, her sincerity tugging at his heart with an undeniable force. From the moment he'd laid eyes on Betsy Anderson he'd felt something. Something strong. Something primal.

"*I* could," he said, his voice taking on a husky tone even to his own ears.

She tilted her head to look at him, squinting in confusion. "I don't understand."

"I think a kiss might make it even better." Inhaling deeply, he cupped the back of her head with his hand and leaned across the center console, his mouth finding hers as a soft moan escaped her lips.

Chapter Four

She walked from room to room, soaking up every detail of the cottage. The kitchen and its adjacent hearth room were warm and inviting with their pale yellow walls and clean white baseboards. The master bedroom on the opposite end of the house boasted neutral colors as did the spare room that would serve as Betsy's office. But it was the sunporch off the back of the house that would be where she'd write during the day as the afternoon sun danced across her keyboard.

There was no doubt about it, she was excited—excited to be embarking on a new book, excited to feel the kind of motivation she'd been lacking for entirely too long, excited at the prospect of rebuilding her life in a place where memories weren't waiting around every corner. Yet there was another layer of excitement that burned every bit as strong as all of those.

And the reason for that layer lived right next door.

Inhaling deeply, Betsy walked onto the sunporch and stopped at the window that afforded the best view of Kyle Brennan's modest home, her thoughts traveling back to the unexpected kiss he'd bestowed on her the night before. The kiss itself had been like none she'd ever experienced, the feel of his lips igniting the firework cliché she'd only read about in romance novels.

But clichés became clichés because of their unshakable place in reality, right? The fact it had never been *her* reality didn't matter.

At least that's what she'd always thought.

Until last night.

Suddenly, the instant attraction and magnetic pull so many of her friends reported when meeting their perfect match didn't seem so far-fetched. She just hadn't realized how all-consuming that kind of attraction could be in a person's life. Nor how many times a warning bell could ring in some recess of her brain when she revisited the kiss in her thoughts.

It wasn't that Kyle Brennan wasn't gorgeous, because he was.

It wasn't that he was missing a few soft edges, because he wasn't. His interaction with his daughter was proof positive of that.

And it wasn't that he was a bum, because that wasn't the case, either. One only had to look at the way he kept the exterior of his home to draw that conclusion.

What he was, though, was a police officer—a man who was trained to put his life on the line. Caring for someone in that kind of profession had nearly destroyed her once. Opting to put herself in that position again— with a man who actually stirred real passion inside her for the first time in her life—would be nothing short of reckless. With a healthy dose of stupidity on the side.

Then again, Kyle Brennan was a police officer in Cedar Creek, Illinois, a town that seemed as far from crime-ridden as one could possibly get.

Shaking her head free of the sensation of his lips on hers, Betsy tried to concentrate on the laptop she'd placed on the oak table in the middle of the room. In the time span of twenty-four hours she'd gone from a writer with no ideas to one who not only had an idea but the motivation to bring it to life on her computer screen.

All she had to do now was sit. And write.

The sound of a soft, yet persistent knock propelled her from the room. As she approached the front hallway, a smile stretched across her face at the sight of the child on the other side of the screen door.

Dressed, once again, in a brown vest and matching beret, Callie Brennan happily waved a sheet of paper in Betsy's direction while rocking from heel to toe on her sneakers. "Hi, Miss Anderson! Guess what I have?"

Betsy stepped outside. "I don't know…what?"

Callie jumped up and down, her excitement making the sheet of paper in her hand bounce along with the rest of her. "I have my order form this time. So you can mark the exact cookies you want."

"What a good little salesperson you are." Betsy reached outward, bypassing the order form just long enough to tuck a strand of hair back behind Callie's ear. Once it was in place, she looked down at the paper in the little girl's hand. "Ooh, look, there's pictures of the cookies to tempt me even further."

"That's what my leader said, too," Callie exclaimed as her jumping morphed into a hop from foot to foot. "She said people can't…re…resip cookies."

"Resip?" Betsy repeated.

"She said when people see a picture of a cookie they can't resip them."

"Oh, you mean, *resist*."

The child nodded, her face serious. "Wow. I bet you never make mistakes with words. My grandma says you must be really smart to write a book."

Squatting down beside Callie, Betsy met her awed gaze head-on. "I make mistakes all the time. Everyone does. It's how we learn, whether we're big or little. And as for being smart, I think smart comes in lots of packages. Mine just happens to be in a package wrapped with my imagination."

"Imagination?" A dimpled smile lit Callie's face as Betsy's words sunk in. "That's what you need to be a writer?"

"It's one of the most important things, yes."

"My grandma says I have that all the time! Daddy does, too."

Betsy tapped a gentle finger on the tip of Callie's nose. "And you like to write poems, right?"

"Uh-huh."

"Then it sounds to me like you and I are both writers."

A squeal erupted from Callie's mouth that made Betsy laugh, the child's enthusiasm for writing tickling her own. "You really think so?"

"I know so." She glanced down at the order form once again, her finger gliding down the list of options. "Hmm, they all look so good. Which ones did you try at your meeting yester—"

The honk of an approaching car cut her off midsentence and she looked up. A black sport utility vehicle slowed to a crawl before pulling into the Brennans' driveway. Callie squealed again. "Daddy's home!"

Feeling her face warm at the notion of seeing Kyle once again, Betsy stood and waved, her smile slipping from her face as Callie's father stepped from the car in full uniform. In an instant she was standing in the doorway of her apartment, a uniformed member of the NYPD and the captain of Mark's firehouse informing her of her husband's death. He was a hero, they'd said. He'd died a hero's death.

Only she'd never gotten to say goodbye.

Her stomach lurched as, one by one, her senses traveled back to a night she longed to forget—the dimly lit hallway outside her apartment, the acrid smell of smoke that still clung to the captain's skin, the taste of bile that rose in her throat as they spoke of her husband's heroism….

She grabbed the porch railing in front of her as her knees began to buckle, Kyle's confident stature registering somewhere in her subconscious.

"H-hi," she stammered as Callie ran down the steps and wrapped her arms around her father's legs.

Pausing midstep to greet his daughter, he lifted Callie off the ground and spun her around before setting her back down with a kiss on her forehead. "So how's my girl this afternoon? How was school?"

"It was great, Daddy. We're making a surprise in art class."

"A surprise? Hmm, should I guess?" he asked with a teasing lilt as he peered over Callie's head and winked at Betsy.

"No! Surprises aren't meant for knowing." Callie rested her hands on her hips and leveled a look of distaste at her father. "Trying to guess is like cheating. You know that, Daddy."

She knew she should say something, anything to acknowledge the curious way in which Kyle peered at her in between bantering with Callie, but she couldn't. There was simply nothing in her thoughts except memories—painful, time-stopping memories.

"Why don't you go tell Grandma I'm home and that

I'll be inside in just a minute." Kyle kissed his daughter on the head once again.

"But Miss Anderson is ordering cookies."

Betsy looked down at the order form now wrinkled inside her hand, Kyle's response breaking through the white noise in her head. "Go on and tell Grandma and then you can come back over and get your form."

"Okay." The child scampered across the yard and up the driveway, her white-and-pink sneakers smacking softly against the asphalt. "I'll be right back!"

"We'll be here." Kyle turned his attention from a retreating Callie to Betsy and smiled, his long legs making short work of the distance between them. "I wanted a chance to talk to you alone…if you hadn't already figured that out."

Betsy stood rooted to the front porch. "Is there something wrong?"

"I can't really discuss it too much at the moment, but I can say that we think your observation about the perp from the bank is right on the money."

"My observation?"

He nodded. "Yeah, about his on-camera actions seeming quite deliberate. Looks as if we've got far more on our hands than a thwarted bank robbery."

The sound of metal smacking against wood echoed across the yard signaling Callie's impending return.

"Is it bad?" she asked.

Kyle shrugged. "Yeah, it could be. But—" he gestured toward his daughter "—I don't want to talk about it in front of her. I don't want to scare her."

She managed what she hoped was a nod in the absence of words but it was an effort of mammoth proportions.

He looked at her strangely. "You okay?"

Again she nodded.

Glancing over his shoulder at his daughter, who'd stopped to pick a flower from the front landscaping, he looked back at Betsy, his voice softening. "I was thinking about you today. Specifically about what happened in the car last night. And I was wondering if maybe you'd like to catch a movie tonight?"

He stepped closer and onto the porch, his various police insignia and medals gleaming in the sun.

"I—I—" She stopped, swallowed and tried again, the thudding in her chest nearly drowning out the sound of her own voice. "I can't. I have to write."

She felt his eyes studying her and she looked away.

"Okay, then how about another night? Maybe tomorrow or sometime over the weekend? Would that work?"

Betsy shook her head, the barrage of sensations and memories jelling with a reality she couldn't deny. Kyle Brennan was, by all appearances, a nice guy and a good father. For anyone else, he'd be worth pursuing. But not for her.

She couldn't do it. She simply couldn't do it again. Small town cop or not, his profession came with danger....

"I'll be writing every day. It's the only way I'm ever going to be able to get back home where I belong."

In an instant the smile that had lit Kyle's face was gone, in its place a dark cloud.

"I'm back, Daddy." Callie hopped up onto the porch and extended her left hand shyly in Betsy's direction. "I brought you a daffodil, Miss Anderson. You can put it in the middle of your writing table."

Kyle's hand closed down on his daughter's shoulder,

pulling her backward as his words bit through Betsy's heart. "I think it's high time we left *Miss Anderson* alone. Seems the hustle and bustle is calling."

Chapter Five

He slammed his locker shut, his fist repeating the sound with an even louder bang.

"Yo, dude, what's your problem? You've been a real drag all morning." Tom popped a handful of sunflower seeds into his mouth and leaned against the row of floor-to-ceiling lockers on the opposite wall. "One minute you're surly and silent, the next you're bitchin' about everything from the new flashlights the chief just issued to the speed of the computer out in the hall."

"There is no speed with that piece of garbage."

"Ladies and gentleman of the jury, I present Exhibit A," Tom said as he waved his hand with a flourish toward his partner.

"Exhibit A?"

"Yeah. Your bitchin'."

"Shut the hell up, would you?" Kyle Brennan exhaled loudly as he raked a hand through his hair. "I've just got some stuff on my mind, that's all."

"Callie sick?"

"No."

"Your mom sick?"

"No."

"Heard from Lila?"

He stared at Tom.

"I take that as a no?" Tom popped a few more seeds into his mouth. "Does this have something to do with Betsy Anderson?"

His mouth grew dry. "Why would it?"

"Man, I'm really starting to lose it, aren't I?" Tom leaned forward to rest his elbows on his thighs. "What was that…four? Used to get it on the first try every time. Then again, Lila was an easy guess back then."

Kyle banged the back of his head against the locker behind him.

"Whoa, take it easy there, Ky."

"Can we just not do this right now?" Bending his leg at the knee, Kyle pushed off the row of lockers and strode toward the door that led from the department's locker room to the hall beyond. "I put out some feelers today and I think we're right on the money with our perp. Seems he and his fellow bank robber were working on building themselves a gang a few towns over. Like-minded thugs interested in scoring money for drugs and partying. They figured that if they could get away with the hardware store and the market…maybe they could score a third time with the bank."

Tom rose from his bench but didn't fall into step with Kyle. Instead, he simply stood, feet spread wide, arms folded across his chest. "We squashed that thought, didn't we?"

"If it's just the two of them."

"You seriously think there's more?"

"Two people hardly make a gang."

"True. And it makes sense. But maybe we shut them down at their main artery," Tom suggested in his usual positive way.

Kyle bypassed the closed door and began pacing. "Maybe. Or maybe we pissed them off."

"It's kinda weird how that news footage took on different meaning the more we watched it yesterday. Did you tell Betsy we think she was right?"

He spun around and walked in the other direction. "*Elizabeth Lynn* Anderson is too busy for such small town nonsense."

"What are you talking about? Betsy isn't like that… you know that." Tom's confusion was etched in his forehead. "Hell, you, yourself, were singing her praises all day yesterday. What changed?"

"*She* did," Kyle hissed.

"How?"

"She took off the mask."

"Mask?"

"Hell yeah."

"And?"

"She talks a good game, but when push comes to shove she has no use for a town the size of Cedar Creek."

Tom snorted. "Give me a break, Kyle. She chose to write here, didn't she?"

"Maybe. But this isn't her home."

"I don't know what's eating at you, dude, but you need to chill out."

He stopped, stared at Tom for a moment, and then headed back toward the door, his hand stilling on the knob just long enough to utter a single sentence in response. "The only thing I need to do is keep my daughter away from that woman—far, far away."

BETSY STARED AT THE BLINKING cursor in the top left corner of her still-empty screen, unable to think of a single word. All night long she'd tossed and turned, her latest encounter with Kyle making a continuous loop through her thoughts, the memory of her rude behavior broken only by images of their kiss and the details behind the demise of his marriage to Callie's mother.

She could pinpoint, with absolute clarity, the moment she'd pushed him away. By emphasizing she belonged in New York, she'd likened herself to Kyle Brennan's ex-wife—a woman who thought Cedar Creek was nothing more than a mere stumbling block to a better life.

Betsy rose from her chair and wandered to the window that overlooked Kyle's house. She could still see the look on his face as if she'd slapped him with her words. And she cringed at the memory of Callie's surprise as her father jerked the order form from Betsy's hand and ushered her away.

She'd been wrong. She knew that now. Not about her feelings where Kyle's profession was concerned but, rather, in the way she'd cut him off, making it sound as if Cedar Creek was merely dirt on the bottom of her shoes. She liked this town, liked the people she'd met so far. And she especially liked Kyle and his daughter, Callie.

Determined to make amends at least as far as her rudeness went, Betsy stepped outside and headed in the direction of Callie's house.

"This one's about the sun. And the way it makes me happy when it lights up the sky." Callie began reading from the paper in her hand, a wrinkled page covered in large, careful handwriting. When she was finished, she looked up at Betsy. "Did you like that one, too?"

Betsy smiled as she tucked her legs underneath her

body on the wicker settee. "It was wonderful. I liked the way you referred to the sun as the big warm circle in the sky. Very nice, Callie."

The little girl beamed as she set her paper on top of the pile of similarly wrinkled papers between them. "I've got one more...this one's 'bout my grandma because I don't have a mom—not really, anyway. And my teacher said we had to write one about someone special to us."

"What about your dad?"

"My teacher said it could only be half a page. My dad would take up more than that."

Her throat constricted as the little girl's earnest words took root in her heart. If Callie felt a sense of loss at not having a mother, it didn't show. "You could write one now if you wanted."

"You mean, outside of school?"

The surprise in Callie's voice made Betsy laugh. "Of course. All you need is paper and a pencil, right?"

"Right!"

"And after you write it, we could put all of these—" Betsy lifted the pile of poems into the air then set them back down "—into a little booklet."

"Could we make a cover? So it looks like a real book?" Callie asked, her eyes large.

"A book of poetry—*your* poetry."

Callie pointed at the stack of poems she'd read to Betsy. "Could I rewrite all of those? I dropped my writing folder on the floor of the bus the other day and someone stepped on it. That's why they're so messy. And if I did them over, I could work extra hard to make my writing look neat and pretty."

"Sure. I think that's a great idea, though your handwriting looks neat and pretty to me already."

The slam of a car door made them both look up. "Oh no, it's Daddy! I wanted to get started on his poem."

Betsy dropped her feet to the ground as Kyle headed in their direction, a slash of anger where a smile had been just the day before. "Why don't you go inside? I have paper and pens on the sunporch. You can get started while I talk to your dad for a few minutes."

"Do you have any pencils? 'Cause I make mistakes."

"They're in with the pens…I make mistakes, too."

"Okay." Callie scooted off the settee, her voice dropping to a whisper. "Don't tell Daddy 'bout my surprise, okay?"

Clamping her lips shut, Betsy curved her thumb and index finger against her lips and turned it in a locking motion. "Your secret is safe with me."

As the little girl disappeared inside, Kyle's pace quickened. "Where is she going?"

"She's working on a surprise. For you."

He stepped onto the porch, his uniform from yesterday replaced by a pair of jeans and a Chicago Cubs shirt. "She can work on a surprise at home."

Betsy placed a gentle hand on his chest as he approached the door, the feel of his skin beneath hers unleashing the butterflies in her stomach. "Please, I want to help her with this. It was my fault she was upset yesterday afternoon and I'm sorry about that."

"My daughter is none of your concern."

She winced at the anger in his voice but stood firm. "I'd like her to be."

"She doesn't need you riding in, trying to fill some void you perceive in her life only to turn around and ride out as quick as you can. She's fine."

"A void? In her life?" Betsy jerked her head in the

direction of the closed door and held a finger to her lips
to quiet his rising voice. "I'd be blind not to see that's
one well-adjusted little girl in there. If there's a void in
someone's life...it's mine."

Shock chased anger from his face. "Yours?"

She shrugged. "I've felt more pangs of healing in
the three days I've been in this town than in the twelve
months prior in New York. And spending time with
Callie...talking about her poetry and listening to her
innocent observations on the world around her is healing. *For me.*"

"I don't know what to say."

"Then don't. Just accept my apology for being rude
yesterday. It's what I was coming over to tell you when
I found Callie on my front porch. My rudeness wasn't
a reflection of anything you did or didn't do. Not the
you that's standing in front of me right now, anyway.
It's what comes along *with* you...when you're dressed
the other way."

She met his gaze, felt her defenses cracking at the
raw emotion splayed across his face. "Dressed the other
way? What does that— Wait! You don't like the fact that
I'm a cop?"

"I admire the fact that you're a police officer. I respect what you've decided to do with your life but it's
what comes with—"

Callie appeared on the other side of the door, her face
stretched nearly ear to ear by a grin that magnified the
sapphire-blue eyes she shared with her father. "Daddy,
guess what?"

She felt his eyes leave her face, swallowed at the
break in the scrutiny as he addressed his daughter with
an air of distraction. "What's that, pumpkin?"

"Miss Anderson put my flower exactly where I said. It's right next to her computer."

"Of course I did." Betsy matched Callie's smile with one of her own. "The color reminds me to be happy."

"You need a reminder?" Kyle asked.

"Sometimes, yeah." And it was true. Though, for some reason, happiness was coming a little easier since arriving in Cedar Creek.

For a long moment he simply studied her, the sudden silence between them anything but awkward. When he finally spoke, he addressed Callie with his words while maintaining his visual focus on Betsy.

"I was thinking, Callie, about those hamburgers and hotdogs we bought the other day. The pretzels, too. What do you say we have a barbecue tonight and invite Tom and Ang to join us? Miss Anderson here, too…if she can put aside her writing for a few hours."

Callie's squeal escaped the screen between them, her enthusiasm matched only by the sound of her feet as they jumped up and down. "Can you? Can you, Miss Anderson? My daddy makes the best hamburgers *ever.*"

A deep breath chased away the parade of fears that threatened to answer for her. Betsy winked at Callie before looking back at Kyle. "The best burgers *ever?* Wow…with an endorsement like that, how could I even think about declining?"

Chapter Six

She knew she was staring but she couldn't help herself. In or out of uniform, there was no denying the fact that Kyle Brennan was a good-looking man. Though, in all fairness, she wouldn't mind seeing what he looked like with absolutely nothing on.

Feeling her face warm at the thought, Betsy returned her attention to the version flipping burgers in front of her rather than the version in her fantasies. The man at the grill was an alluring mixture of confidence and approachability with a healthy dash of both playfulness and sincerity.

"Pretty easy on the eyes, isn't he?"

Startled, she looked up as Angela dropped down on the picnic bench beside her, her face flushed from an intense game of one-on-one volleyball with her husband. "What are you talking about?"

Angela jerked her head in the direction of the grill. "The host."

"I'm not sure I know what you mean." She knew the words were lame, the believability behind them laughable, but she gave it a shot anyway.

"You know exactly what I mean. You've been eyeing

Kyle for the past ten minutes. I know it. Tom knows it. And Kyle knows it."

She gripped the edge of the picnic table as her mouth grew dry. "You think he knows?"

Rolling her eyes skyward, Angela reached for a chip from the brimming bowl in front of them. "You think most men naturally flex their muscles while lifting a beer bottle or handling a spatula?"

She laughed in spite of her embarrassment. "You think that was for my benefit?"

"Judging by the way he watched you from the corner of his eye every time he did it...I'd say, yeah." Angela considered the half-eaten chip in her hand before popping it into her mouth. When she was done chewing, she continued. "And judging by the way you were watching every move he made, I'd say he was successful in his mission."

"His mission?" Betsy rested her head on her fist and grinned at her new friend. "You think he has a mission?"

"Do pigs fly?"

She laughed. "Actually, no."

"Oh, sorry. Bad analogy." Angela looked around the Brennans' backyard, her eyes stopping on the swing set where Callie was happily doing tricks on the monkey rings for Tom. "Is Callie Brennan cuteness personified?"

Lifting her head from her hand, Betsy looked from Angela to Callie and back again. "You're *that* sure he's trying to impress me?"

"And then some." Retrieving another chip, Angela held it out to Betsy, who shook her head, prompting Angela to make a face before happily munching away.

"This is exactly why the chubby get chubbier and the thin stay thin. Anyway…is it working?"

Her gaze traveled back to the grill and the man standing in front of it, a beer bottle in one hand, a spatula in the other. "Is what working?"

Angela's hearty laugh got Kyle's attention but not before he caught Betsy looking and flashed a knee-weakening smile in her direction. "Hey, just because I'm slaving over this hot grill doesn't mean I should be left out of all the fun. What's going on over there?"

"Nothing more than two chicks ogling the chef."

Betsy felt her mouth gape open, her face flame red. Looking down at the table she peeked up through long lashes to find Kyle sporting an aura of satisfaction. To Angela she gasped, "What are you doing?"

"Giving things a little nudge."

"What things?"

"You and Kyle. You're perfect together."

She widened her eyes in mock horror.

"Oh, c'mon… Handsome, yet skittish cop. Beautiful, yet wounded next-door neighbor. You couldn't write it better yourself, Betsy." Angela dug her hand back into the bowl. "But being the impatient reader I am, I want you two to skip straight to the good parts."

"Good parts?" Tom asked as he plopped down on the bench across from them. "What good parts?"

She shook her head at Angela but it was too late. "The hot and heavy date, the wildly intense sexual buildup."

"Whoa, now. What'd I miss?" Tom looked from Angela to Betsy and back again before looking over his shoulder at Kyle. "You could have told me I was missing this kind of conversation, dude."

Exhaling a soft groan of embarrassment, Betsy rested

her forehead back on her hand as Kyle's voice tickled her ears. "I was too busy trying to follow it for myself, partner."

She dropped her head all the way onto the table.

"Daddy, you better hurry up with those hamburgers... Miss Anderson looks mighty hungry." Callie's soft little hand stroked the side of Betsy's cheek, her eyes rounding as she did. "And maybe get out the sprinkler because she seems really hot."

Where's the rewind button when you need it?

"No 'seems' about it." The huskiness of Kyle's voice and the meaning behind his words made Betsy lift her head just in time to see Angela's thumb shoot up at Tom in a celebratory gesture. "Now, who's ready for a burger and a dog?"

Tom leaped to his feet, stopping only long enough to hike his shorts upward on his rounded form. "Don't have to ask me twice."

"C'mon, Miss Anderson. You're gonna love my daddy's burgers. They're really, really yummy."

"Just like Daddy," Angela quipped devilishly, her voice just loud enough for Betsy's ears.

IT WAS HARD NOT TO NOTICE how well Callie and Betsy hit it off, their rapport one of mutual admiration and interest—Callie intrigued by Betsy's career, Betsy fascinated by Callie's...

Youth?

Sweetness?

He wasn't entirely sure.

Kyle turned the scraper in his hand and pushed it against the wire rack, his attention on the mismatched volleyball game in front of him. Or, rather, the woman in the white shorts and yellow halter top who had teamed up with his daughter to take on the Murphys.

His gaze followed the soft curves of Betsy's body as she stood poised and ready at the net, lingered on the long shapely legs that darted around Callie with ease. Oh, what he wouldn't give to have those legs wrapped around him.

"You gonna keep messin' with that grill or are you gonna get out here and play?" Tom's voice carried across the lawn before being cut off by a stray ball to the face. "Whoa now."

Callie's giggle propelled him from the grill, his desire to spend time with her met only by his desire to be as close to Betsy as possible. Jogging over to the net, he took his place behind his next-door neighbor as she waited for the ball, his attention stolen from the game by the way her shorts framed her—

Whump.

Kyle staggered backward, his hand holding his head.

In an instant Betsy was at his side, her long slender hand pulling his backward. "Are you okay?"

He inhaled her scent, an alluring mixture of violets and soap that got his heart thumping and his body reacting.

"That's what you get for not keeping your eye on the ball where it belongs, dude." Tom didn't even bother hiding his smile as he flashed a knowing look at Kyle. "Your eyes need to be focused on game-level not—"

"Yeah, I got it, Tom," he said, cutting his partner off midsentence but not before catching a note of curiosity on Betsy's face. To her, he said, "Shall we take them down?"

Her mouth tugged upward in a conspiratorial smile that nearly rocked his world. "Oh, yeah."

For the next ten minutes the two of them dashed around in pursuit of the ball, high-fiving one another as spike after spike left their opponents speechless. More than a few times Betsy bumped into him while moving back for a volley—a contact he could have avoided but opted not to. Every time it happened he felt his body react, hoped and prayed she didn't notice. Her laughter was intoxicating, making his head spin with a level of desire that was foreign yet undeniably exciting.

There was no doubt about it. Betsy Anderson stirred things inside him. Things that would be best explored in private...with candles burning...soft music playing... and no one around for miles...

Whump.

Again, her hands were on him, the feel even more heady than it had been the first time thanks to the images that had been playing in his mind since the game started. "You're going to be black and blue by the time this game is over."

"Nah, I'll be—"

"Gotta keep your eyes on the ball *and* your head in the game, dude."

"My head *is* in the game," he countered as he shook off the latest ball strike.

"Not in this game it ain't." Tom looked at his watch and then his wife, his teasing grin turning to one of affection. "It's getting kind of late. What say we wrap this up and head home?"

Angela looked as if she was about to protest until she followed the direction Tom's not so subtle eyebrows were indicating. Kyle grinned. There were times Tom was a bit thick, slow to get a hint even when it was fairly obvious to everyone else around him. But this time he was getting it before Kyle even gave it.

After the Murphys left, Betsy stayed behind to help shuttle dishes and leftovers into his kitchen, chattering with Callie the whole time. Once everything was inside and put away, she took a step toward the door, a move he stopped with a gentle hand on her arm. "Let me put Callie to bed and then walk you home."

She gazed up at him through thickly lashed eyes, a sweet yet smoldering look that made him wish, for that moment, that he had a nanny. "It's just next door. I won't get lost."

"I know, but I want to walk you home." Turning to his daughter, he felt an entirely different pull on his heart— the kind of pull that made him feel like a superman and a ball of mush all at the same time. "Hey, pumpkin, I think it's time you went off to dreamland, okay?"

"Okay, Daddy." And as easy as that, Callie slipped her hand inside his and led the way down the hall, waving good-night at Betsy before disappearing into her room. After changing into her pajamas and brushing her teeth, she climbed into bed and settled her head on her pillow. Looking up at him, she flashed a sleepy smile. "She's really pretty, isn't she?"

He cocked his head as he smoothed her hair from her face. "Who is?"

"Miss Anderson." Callie yawned, her words growing softer and more difficult to discern. "And she's really, really nice, too."

As his daughter's eyes drooped closed, he bent over and kissed her softly on the cheek. "Yes, she is. On both counts."

Once he was sure his daughter was fast asleep, he headed back out to the living room and a waiting

Betsy, his heart rate accelerating as she came into view. "Thanks for waiting." Placing his hand on the small of her back, he guided her through the kitchen door and out into the now-empty backyard. "I'm glad you came tonight. I really enjoyed having you here."

"I enjoyed being here. I can't tell you the last time I had this much fun."

He stole a glance at her face as they walked between their homes, their bodies fitting easily through a gap in the hedge line. "Any chance you'd be up for some more tomorrow?"

"More what?"

"Fun."

The soft, melodic sound of her laughter brought an instant smile to his lips. "Will there be burgers involved?" she asked.

"Now you sound like Callie." He reached for her arm as they approached her back door, turning her slightly so their eyes met. "I was thinking more along the lines of a picnic at the park for just the three of us. Maybe some sandwiches, some chips, some fruit."

Her hand came down on his, her eyes sparkling in the glow of the moon. "Ooh, let me pack it. To repay you for such a nice time tonight."

"Your smile is all the payment I need."

She blushed. "Please. I'd like to do this."

"Okay. Say three o'clock?"

"You don't have to work tomorrow?" she asked.

"I've got a six-to-two tomorrow. But enough about that…" He stepped closer, reveled in the feel of her body in such close proximity to his own. Lifting her chin with his fingers, he closed his mouth over hers, felt the sensuous heat as his tongue slid between her lips—teasing, exploring, tasting. Their tongues danced with one another as she molded against him, her arms snaking around his neck as his hands found her tiny waist. He pulled her toward him, wanting her to feel his attraction, to know—beyond a shadow of a doubt—how much he wanted her at that moment.

Finally she pulled away, the longing in her eyes surely a mirror of his own. "You need to get back…to Callie. But I'll see you both tomorrow."

He reached out, held her face in his hand as he soaked up every detail of her expression, committing it to memory. "I can hardly wait."

Chapter Seven

Betsy padded into the kitchen, her pink slippers making a soft tapping sound on the linoleum. For the first time in months she'd slept through the night, hope winning out over the nightmares and regrets that ordinarily drove her from bed before dawn. And it was all because of Kyle Brennan.

Or, rather, the slack she'd finally cut herself where he was concerned.

He was fun.

He was sweet.

He was a loving and attentive father.

He was accomplished at the grill.

He was gorgeous.

And he was an amazing kisser.

Closing her eyes, she leaned against the counter and inhaled the memory of his lips on hers, savored the passion that fired between them as their backyard goodbye had threatened to become an all-night affair. The verbal details of their impending picnic in the park had melted on their tongues as his lips strayed from hers in search of her chin, her neck, her shoulders—a methodically sensual exploration that had been cut short by a strange sound behind Kyle's house.

In a split second their moment had ended, Kyle's hand finding hers for a quick squeeze before running back toward his home and Callie. What the sound was, or what exactly had caused it, she didn't know. But what she did know was simple.

She was falling for Kyle Brennan.

Officer Kyle Brennan.

Was she crazy for allowing herself to get tied up with a police officer—a person who swore to protect the public at all cost? Was she insane to put her heart on the line once again—knowing that this time it was actually engaged?

Probably. But being a police officer in Cedar Creek, Illinois, was a far cry from its big-city counterpart. Here, people left their doors unlocked at night. Here, people retired for the evening when the sun went down. And here, everyone knew everyone.

It was okay. Falling for Kyle Brennan was okay.

She peered at the microwave clock, making note of how long she had before being with Kyle again. Six hours would be more than enough time to get a little writing in, get herself showered and dressed and to prepare a picnic lunch that would appeal to both Callie and her dad.

The ring of her cell phone put an instant stop to the mental inventory of her refrigerator, the jingle it boasted signaling a call she couldn't ignore.

Marsha Greene had been her editor since day one with Yorkshire Publishing and, for the most part, it had been a relationship of mutual respect. Lately, though, things had been different and it was Betsy's fault.

Lifting the phone from her purse, she flipped it open and held it to her cheek. "Good morning, Marsha."

"Betsy."

"What can I do for you today?"

"You can tell me when you'll deliver your next book so I can stop looking at the floor every time my boss asks me that question."

She could hear the stress in the woman's voice and rushed to reassure her. "You'll have it on your desk in six months."

"Six months is much too long, Betsy. Especially for a book we should have had six months ago."

"Marsha, I've been trying. I just didn't have anything that could come close to what you need from me."

"And now you do?"

Betsy sat in front of her computer and opened the file that would, eventually, be her next novel. Other than her name and address in the top left corner, she had nothing.

Not on paper anyway.

"Yes, I do. It's been percolating in my mind almost nonstop the past few days and I think I'm ready to go."

"Then go. I'll be expecting it on my desk by the first of August."

She rolled her mouse over the calendar icon on her toolbar and clicked, the year-at-a-glance feature causing a reflexive swallow. "That's three months away."

"Yes, it is."

A slew of protests sprang up inside her throat only to be swallowed back down. She'd only herself to blame after her nearly yearlong pity party. Now it was high time to put an end to the festivities and begin the long-awaited cleanup process on her life.

Squaring her shoulders, she inhaled deeply, determined not only to get back in the game but also to win one for the team. "You'll have it on your desk by the first of August."

"BRENNAN, MURPHY…IN HERE, *now*."

Kyle glanced at his partner as they stopped, in unison, outside the lieutenant's door, the man's bluntness as much a given around the department as off-color jokes and tall tales. In fact, it was the rare occasion when their boss was polite that they had reason to worry.

"Lieutenant, you're looking well."

"Shut your piehole, Murphy."

"I'll do that, sir." Tom threw his shoulders back as he clicked his heels and came to parade rest.

Kyle rolled his eyes then cut to the chase. "What's up, Lieutenant?"

"My antennae…as should be yours, Brennan." Doug Grady pushed his chair back and stood, his stance one of tension. "We've got a problem."

"A problem?" He stole a glance at his partner, confirming that he, too, was clueless as to the direction of this particular conversation.

"Rumblings have been called to the department's attention."

"Come to think of it, I could use some food myself." Tom smacked his hand into Kyle's arm. "Hot dogs sound good to you, Ky?"

Shaking his head, he kept his attention focused solely on the lieutenant as reality overshadowed his friend's futile attempt to lighten the mood. "Does this have something to do with the perp from the bank?"

Doug raked a hand through his crop of salt-and-pepper hair, nodding as he did. "You were right. About all of it. The two of them were part of a gang. One that appears to have fairly long-reaching arms."

"How long?"

"Long enough to keep you on your toes, Brennan." The lieutenant walked over to the window that over-looked Cedar Creek's town square and spun around, his gaze a mixture of anger and concern. "Word on the street has it that you ruined their fun. And now they're wanting to repay the favor."

"Repay the favor?" Tom repeated.

Doug ignored Tom's question and focused, instead, on Kyle. "Home number still in your mother's maiden name?"

He shifted foot to foot, his stomach tightening as the implications of his boss's words took root. "Yes, sir."

"You have a security system in your home?"

"The best kind," he answered as his hand instinctively fell on the handle of his gun.

"But what about when you're not there? Is there a security system wired to your doors and windows?"

"No."

"We're gonna change that."

"We're?" Tom asked.

"The department, Murphy."

"The department, sir?" Kyle echoed.

"That's right, Brennan. When we feel the safety of an officer's family may be in jeopardy, we'll take whatever precautions are necessary to correct the situation."

"You think Callie—" He stopped, his mouth unable to put words to the thought squeezing his heart.

Doug's hand shot up in the air, his palm faced toward them. "We've got no reason to believe they know where you live. But Cedar Creek is a small town. Most people know where our officers live. Whether that information can be coaxed out by a stranger remains to be seen."

"But why Kyle?" Tom asked.

"Because Kyle was the one who arrested one of their own. The one who messed things up for them, so to speak."

"But what about Logan? He cuffed the other one."

The lieutenant waved Tom off. "But Kyle was the one caught in the camera lens with one hand on one of their buddies. And it was *that* perp who was working the camera…sending whatever message he was sending to his fellow thugs."

"Oh, man—" Tom turned to look at Kyle. "Your name tag was in that shot, wasn't it?"

Kyle simply nodded, his mind racing to corral the implications of what he was hearing. Should he send Callie and his mom on a vacation for a while? Should he pack up her dolls and clothes and send her to live with Lila?

The last thought made his teeth clench, his hands fist in anger.

"Look, we've got no reason to believe these guys know where you live or that you have a daughter. None whatsoever. I'm just saying to be aware when you're at home. Keep the security system on when you're not. And if you hear anything…anything at—"

He knew the lieutenant was still talking, could see the man's mouth moving, but it was all lost on Kyle, drowned out by the sound that had cut short his kiss with Betsy less than twelve hours earlier.

At the time it had sounded like a stick snapping under the weight of a body, but when he'd jogged to the break in the hedge between the two properties, there'd been nothing.

Had it truly been a squirrel or a raccoon as he'd justified to himself at the time? Or could it have been someone outside his home…waiting, watching? The thought made him shiver.

"You holding something back, Brennan?" the lieutenant asked sharply.

"I don't think so."

"What happened?"

He looked from his boss to his partner and back again, still unsure whether what he'd heard was something pertinent or absolutely nothing at all. "Last night. I walked my neighbor home after a little backyard barbecue and while we were…while we were saying good-night, I heard a sound. Like someone was walking around my house. But when I looked, I saw nothing. Chalked it up to an animal."

"Maybe it was. And…maybe it wasn't. Let's hope it was the latter but be prepared for the former." The lieutenant dropped back into his chair, planting his elbows on the top of his desk. "Now, get back to work…the both of you."

With barely more than a nod, Kyle followed Tom back into the hallway and out into the parking lot that housed the department's fleet of patrol cars, the chief's warnings replaying their way through his mind. As they reached their car, Tom broke the silence, his usual joke-a-second attitude surprisingly muted. "You okay, dude?"

He shrugged then slid into the driver's seat of the patrol car while his partner took the passenger seat. "At this point it's all speculation—a bunch of ifs. Of course I'll be vigilant for Callie's sake. But I don't even know if that sound I heard last night was an animal or what."

"You mean, the sound you heard while you were—"

Tom's voice changed, morphed into a near dead-on impression of Kyle's "—saying good-night to your next-door neighbor?"

He laughed, his partner's mimic a much-needed break after a tense conversation with their lieutenant. "Betsy is my next-door neighbor and we did say good-night."

"I notice you didn't mention she's also hotter than hell."

Kyle started the car. "I didn't mention the kiss, either."

"Whoa hoa hoa…a kiss?" Tom's hand shot into the air in celebration only to come back down and punch Kyle in the shoulder. "Man, you move fast."

"Fast was the other night…after pizza with you and Ang." He stole a sidelong glance in his partner's direction as he steered the car out of its parking space and toward the main road that led through Cedar Creek. "Last night was much more slow. And hot. And—"

"And I'm just hearing about this *now?*"

"I didn't think I should kiss and tell."

"Like she'd find out?" Tom asked, his voice echoing with stage-worthy indignation.

Kyle stared at Tom. "I love Ang, I really do. But she's not exactly adept at keeping secrets." With anyone else, Kyle would worry that his words would offend. But with Tom, he knew he was safe.

"Because keeping secrets would mean having the ability to keep one's mouth closed."

Kyle laughed. "Something like that."

They rode in silence for a few blocks, each lost in their own thoughts. Finally, Tom spoke, his words jetting Kyle right back to Betsy's back stoop. "Was it good?"

"What?"

"Don't play coy with me, dude. Was it good?"

A knowing smile tugged at his lips as he turned the car onto Gander Street on the western edge of town, his foot instinctively letting off on the gas pedal as they approached the row of empty warehouses that dotted the area. "It was incredible."

"When are you gonna see her again?"

A warm feeling spread throughout his body as the answer succeeded in chasing away the dread ushered in by his lieutenant. "At three o'clock. We're taking Callie to Paxton Park for a picnic."

"Sounds good. I like her…she's a sweetheart."

Tom's description rolled around in his thoughts as they pulled in and out of each and every empty lot, looking for any signs of criminal activity. A favorite spot for restless teenagers and the occasional small-time drug dealer, the derelict warehouses had become a bone of contention during many mayoral races over the past decade.

"Do me a favor when you're at the park today?"

He glanced over at his partner. "Be on my toes? Trust me, I'm already there."

Tom shook his head. "I was thinkin' more the other way."

"The other way?"

"Look, I realize you've got to keep your eye open after what Grady said…I get that. But don't let it ruin the picnic. Use that time to relax. With Betsy."

Tom was right. What the lieutenant said certainly bore consideration and extra vigilance but it didn't have to consume him. Today was about him and Callie…and getting to know Betsy even more.

Inhaling the memory of Betsy's lips on his, Kyle smiled. "Roger that, partner."

"Daddy, can I knock?"

Kyle smiled down at his daughter, the excitement in the little girl's eyes impossible to miss. "Absolutely."

Callie knocked, the sound surprisingly loud against the door. "Did you remember the Frisbee?"

"I did. The wiffle ball and bat, too." He gestured toward the door. "Give it another one, I don't think she heard."

Callie knocked again, this time even louder. Still there was no response.

"Why don't you try the doorbell?" he suggested.

The doorbell, too, went unanswered.

Her eyebrows furrowed as Callie peered up at Kyle. "I thought you said she was coming to the park with us…that she was packing a picnic."

"I did. Because she said she was." Stepping away from his daughter, Kyle peeked through a narrow window beside the door, the empty hallway providing no clues to the woman's whereabouts. Had she fallen ill? Had something happened?

The thought was no sooner through his mind when fear gripped his heart, squeezed it in time with the memory of his lieutenant's words. Stepping to the left, Kyle pressed his face to the window, scanning the small yet tidy living room but to no avail.

"Daddy, is everything okay?"

Waving away his daughter's question, Kyle stepped to the right, his gaze traveling around the front parlor and down a second hallway that led to—

Betsy.

Squinting, he stared at the woman in his sights, her petite body hunched over her laptop as she tapped away at her keyboard, completely oblivious to their presence at her door and their plans to spend the day together….

Was it possible she simply hadn't heard Callie's knock?

He tried again. Still, she didn't move. Didn't look up. Didn't acknowledge his presence in any way, shape or form.

Grabbing hold of his daughter's hand, Kyle fairly dragged her down the stairs and over to his car, anger coursing through his body where anticipation had been just moments earlier.

"Where are we going, Daddy?"

"I told you. Paxton Park." He knew his words were clipped, his tone angry, but he couldn't help it. He was furious.

"But what about Miss Anderson? I thought you said she—"

He yanked the car door open and gestured Callie into the backseat, his reply bringing an end to her parade of questions. "I made a mistake, Callie. About the picnic... *and* about our neighbor."

Chapter Eight

If there was any chance he simply hadn't heard her, it disappeared the moment their eyes locked through the windshield of his car. Kyle Brennan was mad, of that there was no doubt.

But she hadn't intended to forget their date. She'd looked forward to it from the moment he'd asked her to join them at the park, had planned their picnic meal down to the color napkins she would bring. Yet it had all faded away as she sat at the keyboard with Marsha's grueling deadline ringing in her ears.

When she'd started, she'd been aware of the time, planning to write until one and then shutting down for the day. Her intentions had been good, however her execution had been awful. As the words poured from her fingertips she'd gotten caught up in the story that was beginning to unfold.

Before she knew it, the natural light that streamed through the windows of the sunporch had all but faded, the necessity of lamplight failing to alert her to the mistake she'd made—a mistake that hit her between the eyes as she opened the refrigerator for a midnight snack and saw the makings of their forgotten picnic dinner.

In an instant her ravenous hunger had dissipated only

to be replaced by a wave of nausea that left her shaking. She'd considered apologizing right then and there but the midnight hour had convinced her otherwise. Instead, she'd set her alarm for an early-morning wake-up that would allow her to catch Kyle on his way to work. She just hadn't counted on his refusal to hear her out, or to even acknowledge her presence, for that matter.

Her shoulders drooped as she watched him back his car onto Picket Lane and speed away, her apology lodged in her throat so tightly it posed a viable choking hazard. She'd hurt him. That was obvious.

What wasn't quite so obvious was how to fix it short of rewinding the hands of—

"That's it," she whispered as Kyle's car disappeared from her line of vision once and for all. There was nothing she could do about yesterday. She, of all people, knew that. Yesterday was over, done. All she had was today and tomorrow.

Glancing at her watch, she jogged across her front lawn and onto her front porch, a sense of hope propelling her through the door and straight to her laptop which stood open, waiting for another day's work. Only this time she'd set an alarm for noon, a gentle nudge to get showered and dressed for what she hoped would be an apology Kyle Brennan would never forget.

SHE WAS WAITING IN THE backyard when he pulled into the driveway, the sound of his parking brake making her pulse race. For the umpteenth time in the past thirty minutes, Betsy looked around, her gaze taking in the wineglasses for them and the princess cup for Callie.

Everything had come together perfectly right down to the traditional red-and-white checked blanket she'd found on sale at a department store in town. She'd stopped writing long before the alarm had sounded, the promise of seeing Kyle and Callie motivating her to accomplish far more than she'd expected in far less time than she'd planned.

Pushing off the blanket, she ran a nervous hand down the sides of the flowered skirt she'd chosen for their picnic, its tiny lilac flowers a perfect complement to the delicately laced lilac camisole she wore. Ordinarily she might have considered the outfit a bit too dressy for a backyard picnic, but not today. Today's picnic was about so much more than just eating. It was about admitting when you were wrong and making amends to people who mattered. People like Kyle and Callie.

For a moment she remained silent as she watched him walk up the driveway, his attention focused on his feet. There was something about Kyle Brennan that excited and calmed her all at the same time.

Maybe it was the simple fact that his inner confidence and outward strength left her feeling as if nothing would ever go wrong under his watch. It was an aura he exuded in spades.

Today, though, there was more. Like tension and sadness and even worry. Had she caused that? Had her carelessness brought him that much unhappiness?

Exhaling the sudden urge to run the other way with her tail between her legs, she stepped forward, her sudden movement making him jump and reach for his hip. "I'm sorry. I didn't mean to startle you. I—" And then she stopped, the fury in his eyes making her unsure of her words.

For a long moment he studied her, his hand finally falling to his side. "What do you want? Run out of paper or something?"

"Paper? No I…" Her voice trailed off as the meaning behind his statement became crystal clear. He didn't need her to explain anything. He knew she'd missed their outing because she'd been writing.

"Look, Betsy…or Elizabeth Lynn…or whoever you are today…I'm really not in the mood for playing games. Especially with someone who makes up rules to serve her own needs." Kyle stepped around her and headed toward the backyard, his shoulders rigid, his pace quick. She turned in her place and followed his movement with her eyes, the coldness of his words bringing a stab of pain to her chest.

And then he saw it—the blanket, the glasses, the basket, the cutting board, the pan of still-warm brownies. Stopping in his tracks, he said nothing for what seemed like an eternity, her heart thudding inside her ears.

"What's this?" he asked, his voice husky.

"It's my apology for a yesterday I ruined. A yesterday that slipped between my fingers because of sheer carelessness on my part. I stuck my earbuds in, turned on my music and started writing. And I wrote, and I wrote and I wrote." She caught her breath as he turned around, his gaze locked on hers as she continued, the words pouring from her lips of their own volition. "I lost track of time, Kyle. I know how lame that sounds. I know how lame it is to *say* it. But it's the truth. I didn't stop—for anything—until midnight. And when I realized what I'd done, I wanted to come over right then and there and beg you and Callie to forgive me."

"Why didn't you?"

"Because it was midnight and I didn't want to wake you."

"You wouldn't have. I was awake."

She swallowed over the lump that threatened to render her speechless. "I didn't know that. Instead, I set my alarm for five this morning. So I could catch you before you left for work."

He looked away, a pinkish hue appearing in his cheeks.

"But I hurt you. And Callie. I know that. And I can understand why you didn't want to see or talk to me this morning." Sensing a slight break in his rigidity, she took a step forward, the distance between them still too wide. "I realized, all over again, how badly I messed up. But if I've learned one thing in the past twelve months it's that no matter how awful you may feel about yesterday, you can't change it. It's done. All you can do is make today better."

"The past twelve months?" he asked as he cocked his head and studied her, his expression softening as he took in her attire.

Shaking her head, she took another step forward, her voice breaking. "Can we take a rain check on that question?"

"If you'd like."

"I'd like." Taking yet another step, she reached out for his hands, a gesture that was met willingly enough. "I tried to think of picnic foods that you and Callie might like. We could eat it right here where I've spread the blanket…or we could throw it in my car and go to Paxton Park the way you'd intended. I just hope you'll find it in your heart to forgive me and allow me to make it better somehow."

"Callie's not here. She's—" He stopped, cleared his throat and started again. "My mom normally comes here to babysit. That way Callie can come home after school just like her friends do. But after yesterday—well, let's just say I had to send her to my mom's for the day. She's going to spend the night there, too."

Blinking against the instant sting in her eyes, Betsy looked down at her feet. "She hates me, doesn't she?"

A soft laugh made her look up, a genuine thawing evident in Kyle's eyes and stance. "Callie? Hate you? Not even close. She handled your preference for writing in a far more mature way than I did, I'll say that much."

She winced at his choice of words. "It wasn't a preference, Kyle, please believe that. It was nothing more than an oversight. When you write, you tend to get lost in what you're doing sometimes. I know it sounds lame, and I know it's hard to understand, but it happens. And I'm so very, very sorry. For what it's worth, I'd been really looking forward to spending time with you and Callie. But then my editor called and imposed a deadline and I started to write and—" she exhaled a piece of hair off her face, felt it fall back across her forehead undaunted "—I simply messed up. I'm sorry."

"I forgive you."

Her head jerked upward, her mind almost unwilling to believe what her ears heard. "You forgive me?" she repeated.

"I forgive you." Squeezing her hands, he looked over his shoulder, dimples appearing in his cheeks. "Am I smelling fried chicken?"

"Yes."

"And brownies?"

She laughed. "Yes."

"Wine?" he guessed.

"There's wine, but you couldn't possibly smell it."

"I saw the glasses."

"I figured that." Releasing one of his hands, she tugged the other in the direction of the blanket. "And there's crackers and cheese, grapes and mashed potatoes, ice cream—"

"Did you say ice cream?"

"I did."

His eyebrows furrowed. "Won't that melt?"

"That part is in the house. I'll pop over there when it's time for dessert."

He stopped as they reached the blanket, taking her hand as she lowered herself to the ground. "Maybe I'll go with you."

Her cheeks warmed at the implication, a tingle of pure arousal winding its way to every nook and cranny of her body. "That would be nice," she whispered.

The picnic was wonderful, the food a perfect complement to the conversation they shared. He talked about his job and asked about hers. She probed him for department stories and shared some of her craziest book ideas. They talked about Callie and her interest in writing and all things girlish.

"Does she miss having a mother?" she asked, the question surprising even her.

He shrugged. "She doesn't seem to. I try to play both roles."

"You are very good with her."

"Thank you." He touched her face with a gentle hand. "Now may I ask a question? Or, rather, re-ask a question?"

"Sure."

"Earlier, you said you'd learned a lesson over the past twelve months about what you can and can't change in life. Will you tell me more about that now?"

She closed her eyes, inhaling as much courage as she could muster before opening them once again. "I was married before, too."

"Oh?"

"His name was Mark. He was a firefighter in New York City."

"Was?"

"He was killed in the line of duty."

He grabbed her hand. "Oh, Betsy, I'm so sorry. I had no idea."

I'm so sorry...

His words played in her mind, her heart as empty to them as always. She didn't deserve his or anyone else's sympathy. People who grieved their loved ones earned that kind of sentiment. Not people who grappled with guilt.

"We didn't say goodbye when he left that afternoon," she admitted, her voice wooden and stilted. "We didn't say anything to each other, for that matter."

She glanced up at him, expecting to see disgust but found a compassion that encouraged her to go on. "The honeymoon phase only lasted a few weeks before we started drifting apart. It was as if I was just there to fill a role...to be the little woman at home rather than a true partner."

"He was all about the firehouse, wasn't he?"

His question surprised her and she could only nod.

"Some guys are like that. Cops, too. But we're not *all* like that." She closed her eyes at the feel of his finger under her chin, opened them again as he guided her face upward. "Don't get me wrong, my job is important and I take my duty very seriously. But I'm a father, first and foremost. And Callie will never doubt that."

The sincerity with which he spoke made her swipe at her eyes, a futile attempt to stop the threat of tears in their tracks. In an instant his arms were around her, pulling her close, his chin coming to rest on her head as she buried her face in his neck. When her sobs subsided, he put his hands on her shoulders and pushed her away just enough to make eye contact. "The state of your marriage was his responsibility, too, Betsy. But more than that, you have to see that fire was not your fault. Forcing yourself to express a sentiment you no longer felt wouldn't have changed what happened that day. For you or for him. People grow apart. It happens. It happened with Lila and I, too. We wanted different things."

"You wanted a family. She wanted a career."

He seemed to ponder her words as he shifted his position on the blanket and pulled her backward, reclining her body into his. "A simplistic summation, but true nonetheless. And it sounds as if the same was true of your marriage, as well, yes?"

She nodded, his words hitting home in her heart. He was right. Like him, she'd wanted a family—a feeling of connectivity and completion and being one another's priority. But just as the stage had been for Lila, Mark's world had been his department and his badge. "I supported his work as a firefighter, I really did. I admired him for it. It was the other stuff—the constant need to be at the firehouse whether he was on duty or not, the near nightly poker games with the guys at the station, the disinterest in my life—that dragged me down."

"And I supported Lila's dream to be on stage. I just hadn't realized how much she cared about the spotlight and the chance to be a celebrity. It was like a lightbulb switched on inside her when she was on stage…and then turned off the second the attention was gone and she was left with Callie and me."

There was nothing to say to that, nothing to offer other than a nod. They'd both been disillusioned in love, both been pushed aside for something that was seen as more important, more worthy. And they'd both spent entirely too much time second-guessing and regretting. She was about to put words to that thought when she felt his hand snake around her neck and begin caressing her cheek, his lips finding her earlobe and beginning to nibble. The warmth of his body matched her own as she turned to meet his lips with her own, desire heightening with each passing moment.

As their tongues met and explored, she felt his hand slipping down her body, his fingers finding the swell of her breasts. Her sighs were met with a lowering of his hand to her nipples, their hardness pushing against the fabric of her camisole.

He pulled back, grabbing hold of her hand and pulling her to her feet beside him.

"Where are we going?" she asked, her voice breathless.

"I think it's time for that dessert, don't you?"

Her eyes skimmed their way down his body, her throat instinctively tightening at the telltale bulge in his jeans. "I—I have chocolate. And vanilla."

Pulling her against him, he wrapped his arm across her shoulders and walked beside her through the hedge that separated their two homes. "Anything else?"

She was having trouble concentrating. "Ooh, I have mint chocolate chip, too."

"Mmm, sounds good, real good. But it's still not exactly what I had in mind."

As they reached the steps that led to her sunporch, she looked up, her breath catching at the blatant hunger in his eyes. "I don't think there's anything else."

"Oh, yes, there is." Following her up the steps and into the house, he waited as she shut the door, his hands gently pushing her against the wall. "There's you, Betsy."

She gasped as his mouth came down on hers, the longing she'd seen in his eyes paling against the heated passion that ripped through her body as his hand sought the skin beneath her camisole, his fingers twirling her nipples into hard buds and intensifying her longing into moans that echoed against the walls of the room. "Me?" she whispered as her knees began to buckle.

"Yes, you."

Pulling her still closer, she felt his body straining toward hers, knew without a doubt she wanted him just as much as he obviously wanted her. "Kyle…"

He stopped her words with his mouth before lowering his lips to her chin, her neck, her shoulders. When his mouth reached the top of her breasts she knotted her hands in his hair and repeated his name in a whispered moan of ecstasy. "Kyle…I want you."

Chapter Nine

At the time, Callie's good-night call had been the epitome of bad timing, her grandmother's name on Kyle's caller ID bringing an end to their passion-filled night. But now, in the light of day, Betsy couldn't help but see it as a good thing.

It wasn't that she didn't want to sleep with Kyle, because she did. Her body came to life with every stroke of his hand, every nibble of his teeth. But a relationship of that nature, with her next-door neighbor no less, needed to be dictated by more than just their raging hormones.

What had surprised her, though, was the way Kyle had tensed when he realized who was calling, his hurried greeting one of worry rather than a simple hello. And although the call had proved to be nothing more than an opportunity for Callie to say good-night, Kyle's mood was irrevocably altered. Suddenly, where there'd been gentleness there was an edge, where there'd been playfulness there was rigidity, and where there'd been excitement there was restraint.

When she'd asked him about it, he'd been evasive, saying only that there were some things at work that had him on edge—an explanation she could understand if his change in behavior had come on the heels of a phone call from the station. But it hadn't.

A soft knock broke through her woolgathering. Scooping her coffee mug up off the counter, Betsy headed toward the back door, a smile lifting her lips at the sight of Kyle standing on her back step.

"Good morning, beautiful."

She felt her face warm at the compliment, her smile growing still wider. "This is a nice surprise...but aren't you supposed to be at work?"

He shook his head. "Today's my RDO."

"RDO?" she asked.

"Regular day off. I work four, then I'm off two." Kyle stepped inside as Betsy opened the screen door to admit him. "It works out perfect because Callie has a program at school today. Her creative-writing teacher is hosting a reading of the kids' works and Callie, of course, is reading her poetry."

Betsy clapped her hands. "Really? How special!"

"I know. And I can't wait to see her on that stage looking at me the way she does, but..."

"What?"

"Well, we have a little problem."

She reached out, ran her hand through his hair. "What is it?"

He toed the floor, shrugging. "She says she has to look extra pretty to do her reading. I'd thought my mom was going to help her before she dropped her off this morning but she didn't." Crossing his arms in front of his chest, Kyle leaned against the window that over-looked his own backyard. "I tried to help...I even looked in one of the hair books Ang gave me a few months ago, but nothing I do seems to be right."

She tried not to make light of his dilemma yet his

concern was nothing short of endearing. She told him as much.

"Endearing? Really?" His eyes sparkled as he looked at her, his gaze roaming its way down her freshly showered body now clad in a pair of formfitting white jeans and a turquoise-blue halter top.

"Really." Holding her finger upward momentarily, she took a last gulp of coffee before setting her mug down on her laptop table. "Can I help?"

Relief tugged at his shoulders. "I was hoping you'd say that. But—" he gestured toward her computer "—don't you have that deadline to worry about?"

She glanced at the screen behind her, desire winning out over duty. "My writing can wait. Callie is more important."

He flashed his infamous knee-weakening smile then pulled her out the door. "You have no idea how glad I am to hear that. Callie specifically asked for you."

Her skin tingled beneath his hand as it found her lower back and guided her through the now-familiar gap in the hedge, Callie's excited face peeking through the back door at them. "She keeps saying today is a very special day—more special than any other school program she's had."

"Any idea why?" she asked.

Kyle shrugged. "Something about changing the poem she was going to read today to something entirely new… something she just wrote this week."

"This week?"

"That's what she said." Kyle stopped outside the screen door and winked at his daughter. "Isn't that right, Callie?"

Not wanting to ruin the surprise she suspected Callie held, Betsy cocked her head a hairbreadth to the left and smiled at the little girl. "Your personal hairdresser has arrived, Miss Brennan. So what would you like? Braids? Ponytails? Curls? Pretty clips?"

Callie squealed, her hands clapping with excitement. "Curls! Curls!"

She looked at Kyle. "Any chance you have a curling iron handy?"

"As a matter of fact, I do." Gesturing Betsy to follow him inside, he walked five or six feet and then spun around, playfully raking his hand through his hair. "Do you really think I just wake up looking like this?"

"Oh, *Daddy,*" Callie said as she rolled her eyes upward. "You don't use a curling iron. Grandma just left her old one here in case…in case…" A gleam appeared in her eye. "Today just happens to be extra special. And extra special calls for curls and party shoes."

"Party shoes?" Kyle teased.

"And tights, too."

"Anything else?"

Callie appeared to consider her answer carefully, each finger of her right hand extending outward as she ticked off something in her head. "A dress and a hair ribbon would be extra nice. And, oh! I can't forget my poem."

Once her list was clear, Callie grabbed hold of Betsy's hand and pulled. "C'mon, Miss Anderson. I have to hurry."

Kyle bit back his smile as he tried valiantly to replace it with a solemn look. "Yes, Miss Anderson, you really need to hurry."

"I can see that." With a grin and a wave at Kyle, Betsy followed Callie down the hall, her mouth gaping open as the child's room came into view. Somehow, someway, what had surely been an average ten-by-ten room at some point in the home's history had been transformed into a woodland paradise where flowers swayed in the breeze and fairies flew about dispersing their magical dust. Every tree branch, every flower petal, every detail of the dozen or so fairies had been painted with a precise hand and an imaginative eye. In short, it was straight out of a little girl's dream.

Sucking in her breath, Betsy looked around, her eyes noting a detail before her mind had time to fully register the one before. "Oh, Callie," she whispered, "your room...it's beautiful."

"Thank you."

She didn't need to look over her shoulder to know Kyle was there, didn't need his strong voice to alert her to his presence, either. The instant reaction in her body was the only clue she needed. "Who did this?" she asked as she gestured around the room with her hand, her eyes focused, once again, on the breathtaking details. "It's amazing."

"My daddy did it," Callie said as she flopped onto her bed and pointed toward the ceiling. "The clouds, too."

Betsy looked from Kyle, to the ceiling, and back again. "You painted this room? By yourself?"

"I did."

"How long have you been painting?" She heard the shock in her voice, hoped it didn't offend.

"I haven't. This was a first attempt."

"Very funny. Seriously, how long have you been painting like this?"

Kyle exchanged knowing looks with his daughter, his eyes rolling upward at Betsy's disbelief. "Seriously. This was a one-time thing. Callie told me what she wanted and then I tried to sketch it out on paper. She showed me books and posters and even a few dolls—everything and anything she could think of to get me in the know on fairies. Once I got the sketch the way she wanted it, I put it on an overhead, traced it onto the wall and then started painting."

"When did you do this?"

"At night, while Callie was sleeping. I moved her into my room for a few weeks and worked on this once she'd fallen asleep each night."

"It must have taken you months." She felt his eyes on her, knew he was studying her closely, but still, she stared at the mural around her as her mouth tried to put words to her thoughts.

"Yeah, I guess it took about that long. But it was worth it the moment I saw Callie's face. You should have seen the way it lit up when I brought her in here for the very first time." Kyle took a step back. "I suppose I should leave you girls alone to get ready. We need to be at school in—" he glanced at his watch "—about forty-five minutes."

It took every ounce of willpower not to stare at him as he walked away, her heart pounding in her chest. Kyle Brennan was like nothing she'd ever allowed herself to imagine. He conveyed the kind of strength that made a person feel safe—as if by his mere presence bad things simply didn't exist. He was also sexy and tender, the visceral memory of his touch the night before washing over her again. But above all of that, he had a love for his daughter that was as genuine and tangible as any item in Callie's room. It was without question and without doubt.

"Miss Anderson?"

Betsy felt the tug on her hand and looked down, Callie's face hazy.

"Are you okay? You look like you might cry."

She forced herself to smile even as tears burned the corners of her eyes. "I'm fine. You have a really special daddy, Callie."

"I know. And you wanna know something else?"

"What?"

"Pretty soon my whole school is gonna know it, too."

She looked questioningly at the little girl.

"They're gonna know that my daddy is special."

"Oh." She squatted down beside Callie and squeezed her hand inside her own. "Tell me."

"I wrote it."

"Wrote what?" She knew the answer, had sensed it the moment she saw Callie's face, but, still, she wanted to hear it from the horse's mouth.

"The poem. About Daddy. And that's the one I'm going to read today." Pulling her hand from Betsy's, Callie skipped across her room to the little white desk with the baby pink blotter. Moments later she was back, a sparkly purple notebook in her hand. "Can you read it?"

"Now?"

The child's eyes shone with anticipation. "Please."

Slowly she opened the notebook, her attention riveted on the colorful title page.

"I know it's just s'posed to have the name of the poem on it, but I wanted to put pictures there, too." The child hopped from foot to foot, her excitement undaunted by the passage of time. "You know, pictures of Daddy and I doing some of the stuff from the poem…so everyone can see."

Betsy nodded, the lump in her throat making it difficult to talk.

"See that one?" Callie pointed at the drawing on the

upper left corner of the page. "That's us—building sand castles at the beach last summer. And this one—" she tapped her finger on a picture near the bottom "—was from a few weeks ago. I wanted to have a lemonade stand and Daddy helped. He wore the poster I made for his tummy and walked around just like I asked. I made ten whole dollars that day!"

Finally they got to the poem, Callie's hand retreating from the notebook as Betsy began to read. Line by line, the child's words tugged at her heart, made her long for the man seated down the hall—a man she barely knew yet felt as if she did a million times over.

When she finished reading, she closed the notebook and handed it to Callie, her voice raspy with emotion. "Oh, sweetie, that is the most beautiful poem I've ever read."

Callie's eyes widened. "Really?"

"Really." Reaching outward, she pulled the little girl close, inhaling the sweet smell of shampoo and bubble bath that clung to her hair and skin. "Now let's get you ready."

IT WAS OBVIOUS THAT CALLIE'S poem had moved Kyle beyond words. She could see it in the way he'd swallowed repeatedly as his daughter read. She could see it in the way he'd glanced up at the ceiling in an attempt to ward off the tears that glistened in his eyes. And she could see it in the wobbly smile when his hand rose to catch the kiss blown in his direction at the end.

And she was pleased.

By all accounts, single fatherhood had been something he'd neither anticipated nor sought. But rather than shut down or claim ignorance when it was foisted upon him, he'd rolled up his sleeves and thrown himself into the job, raising the kind of child that made people feel good about the world.

Stealing a glance at him across the rapidly filling lunchroom, Betsy couldn't help but feel her attraction deepening. For both him and for Callie.

"Excuse me? But aren't you Elizabeth Lynn Anderson?"

Startled, Betsy turned to find a woman with shoulder-length brown hair staring at her, wide-eyed. Extending her hand outward, she nodded. "Yes, I am."

The woman clapped her hands. "I thought so! I heard through the grapevine that you were renting here in town but I didn't believe it." Turning to a taller woman on her opposite side, she said, "See, Janice? I told you it was her."

And so it went for the next hour as the parents of the students filed into the lunchroom for a reception of cupcakes and punch and stayed for a chance to chat with the novelist who'd come as a guest of Callie Brennan. Callie, for her part, was ecstatic, Betsy's presence at the reading belying any skepticism that had run amuck among the second graders at Cedar Creek Elementary School.

From time to time Betsy would look up, try her best to see if the attention was bothering Callie, but it wasn't. If anything, the little girl seemed even more excited than she'd been that morning, her contagious enthusiasm spreading to everyone around her. Surprisingly, though, Kyle wasn't anywhere to be found.

Curious, Betsy scanned the lunchroom during a break in the crowd, her eyes willing the handsome police officer to appear by her side. Instead, she found him in a far corner, a scowl pulling his mouth downward.

Somehow, in the time that had passed since Callie's poetry reading, Kyle's mood had changed. Gone was the pride etched into his face. Gone was the relaxed stance of his shoulders. And gone was the smile that had drawn her attention to his mouth and her thoughts to places she probably shouldn't be visiting during a school program.

Turning to the last few remaining parents in her circle, she excused herself, her mind already trying to process potential reasons for the change in Kyle's demeanor. Had he gotten a call from work that upset him? Had he had a falling out with a parent in Callie's class? Was he feeling ill?

She headed across the room, Callie at her heels. When they reached Kyle she squeezed his hand, the feel of his skin against hers making the world disappear around them. "Is everything okay over here?"

"I got a call from the department. I really need to get in there as quickly as possible."

The man's tense tone made her uneasy and she glanced down at Callie. Realizing the child was oblivious to the shift in her father's mood, she looked back at Kyle. "Is there something wrong?"

"Looks like it."

In an instant, the peace that had been hers all afternoon was gone, in its place a feeling of dread. "Would it help if I took Callie home with me?"

He shook his head. "No. I want her at my mom's. She'll be safer there."

"Safer?" She drew back. "She's fine with me, Kyle, you have to know that."

He grabbed her hand. "I know she's safe with you. I just don't know she's safe at *your house*."

The dread intensified. "Kyle, what's going on?"

"I can't talk about it now."

"Can't or won't?" she asked.

"Can't."

She willed her voice to remain calm despite the presence of a familiar fear knotting her stomach. "Does this have to do with that guy from the bank?"

A tightening in his jaw confirmed her suspicions.

"Kyle, please…talk to me."

"There's nothing to say. Other than I need to get Callie to my mom's and myself to the station."

"But, Kyle—"

"Betsy, we've gotta go. Can you get yourself home?"

She closed her eyes against the image that suddenly filled her mind—an image she'd replayed countless times over the past year. The police officer standing outside her door, waiting to tell her the kind of news that would shatter her life—her heart—into a million pieces.

"Scratch that. I'll give Tom a call and ask if he can swing by and get you."

Shaking her head, she pulled her purse higher on her shoulder. "I'll be fine. On my own."

And she would be. Disengaging herself was the first step. Sure, she'd be alone again but at least it would be on her own terms.

Chapter Ten

He knew he'd scared her. He saw it in her face—in the way her skin had grown pale and her mouth had tightened as he avoided answering direct questions about the call he'd gotten during the reception at Callie's school.

And after her losing her husband in the line of duty, he even understood it to some degree. But it was a reality of his job she'd have to live with if there was even a chance of a future together.

"So, this phone call that came into the department yesterday. What'd they say, exactly?" Tom asked as he forked up the last bite of scrambled eggs from his plate.

Shaking his head free of all thoughts of Betsy, Kyle concentrated on the topic at hand. "They said they're sick of pigs making rules."

Dropping his fork onto his napkin, Tom pushed his plate to the side. "And what else?"

"They think it's high time the public starts making them instead."

"And by the public, they mean themselves, I take it."

"Lawbreaking dirtbags like themselves...yeah."

"Any idea what these rules might be?"

Kyle stared down at his own plate, his half-eaten breakfast holding little interest. "The only one they mentioned was making me pay."

"For what? Catching them in the act of stealing?" Tom gulped down the rest of his orange juice and jerked his head toward the door to indicate their relief was just about over. It was normally a day off for them, and they were just on patrol to help out a fellow officer whose wife was in labor. "Who the hell are these guys?"

He stood and followed his partner toward the cash register, Tom's words nagging at his soul. Despite the lieutenant's concern, he'd truly believed they'd nabbed the heart of this supposed gang when they thwarted the bank robbery, chalking up any posturing to wounded egos.

But now, he wasn't so sure anymore. The rumblings around town had turned into an actual threat.

One aimed specifically at him.

They stepped outside, the bright morning sun making them both reach for their sunglasses at the same time. "I think I may lose Betsy over this."

"What are you talking about?" Tom strode to their patrol car and yanked open the passenger door. "Why would Betsy walk over a phone call?"

"It's not the phone call, per se. It's the potential it holds."

For a moment Tom said nothing. When he finally spoke, his words hit Kyle with a one-two punch. "Oh. Ang showed me Betsy's Web site. She lost her husband in a fire, didn't she? Well, she, of all people, understands the nature of public service. Give her a chance to digest all of this. Talk to her about it. Maybe, if she feels like she's a part of it, she'll be less scared."

He slid into the driver's seat and shut the door behind him, Tom's suggestion bringing him up short. Had he caused Betsy undue stress by being so vague about the trouble? Would telling her what the lieutenant feared make things less frightening for her?

"I don't know, Tom. I'm a cop. Stuff happens in our job. I can't sugarcoat that for her or anyone else. To do so would be giving her a false sense of security…the way her late husband did when he said he could handle anything. Let's face it, being involved with someone like us is a risk."

"What in life isn't?"

"What do you mean?"

"Every time you give your heart to someone you're running a risk of getting hurt."

He stared at his partner. "That's kinda deep for you, Tom."

"Surprising, I know." Tom shrugged. "But you've gotta get her to the point where you can explain that to her."

"How?"

"You could lighten things up a little."

"Lighten things? How?"

Tom pulled the visor down as they turned into the path of the sun. "You could buy her flowers."

"I can't do that…Callie just gave her some the other day."

"You could buy her candy."

He considered that. "I don't know if she likes candy."

Tom smacked his head against the seat back. "Dude, they *all* like candy. It's their equivalent to our beer gene."

"Beer gene?"

"Yeah. Only they get cranky when they don't get their candy and horny when they do."

"And that's different than us and beer because…" He let Tom get the gist. Besides, they'd strayed from the topic at hand. "Seriously, you think candy will ease her fear?"

"No. But it will let her know she matters to you."

"I don't know… Part of me wants to do whatever it takes to remove that fear I put in her eyes yesterday. But there's also a part of me that wants to be straight up about this."

"Even if it means losing her?"

Raking his hand through his hair, he contemplated his partner's words. There was no denying the fact that Betsy was like nothing he'd ever experienced before. Her warmth, her sweetness, her spirit reached him in a way no one had since…

"Ever," he whispered.

"Come again?"

Realizing he'd spoken aloud, he waved his hand in the air then turned the patrol car into the station's lot and parked in a spot near the door. "I don't know. I was just muttering to myself. But, hey, did the lieutenant say why he wanted to see us?"

"Nah. Just that he wanted our butts in his office as soon as breakfast was over. And to be honest, I didn't feel like engaging him in conversation any longer than necessary."

Glancing at the station house he felt an inexplicable shiver roll through his body. "I'm betting this is about me again."

"Everything doesn't have to be about you all the time, dude. Maybe the lieutenant just wants to give us a well-deserved raise for our undying dedication to the people of Cedar Creek." Tom stepped out of the patrol car and headed across the tarmac to the station, making eye contact over his shoulder every few steps or so. "It is possible, yes?"

Kyle snorted as he followed. "I'll leave that one alone."

The twosome entered the brick one-story building and wound their way around hallway after hallway until they came to the lieutenant's office, a small, impersonal room with a steel-gray metal desk and little else.

"Murphy, Brennan. Nice of you to show up."

"Just finished breakfast, sir."

Doug Grady cast a sidelong glance in Tom's direction before settling his focus on Kyle and pointing at the empty chair across from his desk. "Sit."

Tossing his hat onto his boss's desk, he did as he was told. "What's up?"

"As you know the security system is being installed in your home today."

Kyle nodded. "My mom will be there when they arrive. If they're not done by the time school is over, my mom will take Callie back to her house."

"Good. That system can't get installed soon enough." Doug dropped his hands to his desk and retrieved an envelope from its center. "I want you to make sure it's on when you're home...and when you're not."

He pondered his boss's words. "I've got my gun when I'm home."

"That's added security, Brennan, not primary." Opening the envelope, Doug handed a picture to Kyle. "Who is that?"

His attention dropped to the photograph, his eyes soaking up every detail of the woman standing beside him. It was all there. The long hair, the contagious smile, the body he longed to—

"That's Elizabeth Lynn Anderson," said Tom, rushing to answer the lieutenant's question. "She's Ang's favorite author."

"Okay…but why is she with Brennan?"

Why, indeed.

"She's his next-door neighbor."

He knew they were talking, could hear the exchange happening around him, but he couldn't focus enough to grasp a word. For as hot as Betsy was in person and in the photograph in his hand, there was no denying the fear in her eyes. Fear he was causing simply by being in her life.

"Candy isn't going to cut it," he mumbled.

"Candy cuts everything, dude. Trust me."

"What the hell are you two talking about?" Doug smacked his hand down on the desk. "Look, this is serious. I need to know what her relationship is to you."

The lieutenant's words broke through his disjointed thoughts. "She's my neighbor."

"Is that all?"

He stared at his boss, the shiver from earlier resurfacing down his spine as a troubling picture began to take shape. "I like her."

Tom clapped his hands. "I knew it."

He looked back down at the picture. "She's in danger because of me…isn't she?"

Without a word, Doug Grady reached back into the envelope and removed a sheet of paper. Turning it so Kyle could read the single typewritten sentence that stretched across the top of the sheet, he shoved it toward him. "You tell me."

He leaned forward. Tom did the same.

"Retribution sucks."

His hands tightened at his sides as a burst of anger shot through his body. It was bad enough to consider the possibility that someone might be angry enough to lash out at him for doing his job, but to see it in black-and-white? "Who the hell do these people think they are?"

"Cowboys."

A low whistle escaped Tom's mouth. "Crap. This is getting serious, isn't it?"

"It certainly appears that way."

"How'd they get this picture?"

He stared at the picture, his mind soaking up every detail of Betsy and her surroundings. "They were there yesterday...at the school," he said, clenching his teeth as he slammed his fist into his boss's desk. "This was taken at the damn school."

"Are you sure?"

He pointed at the photograph as he shoved it back in front of the lieutenant. "That's the same outfit Betsy wore yesterday for Callie's reading. And those are the tables that were set up for the cookies and punch afterward."

Jumping up, he strode around the lieutenant's office, his anger intensifying with every step he took. "One of these losers was in my daughter's school...watching me...watching us."

"Jay thinks it's possible it was taken from outside the building, with a high-powered lens."

Jay Rhodes was the department's public relations officer and resident photography expert. If he felt the picture was taken from outside the school it was almost a certainty. Kyle felt his shoulders relax a hairbreadth.

"Which is good on some levels, bad on others."

He turned to face his partner. "What do you mean?"

Leaning against the wall, Tom crossed his arms and released a breath that echoed around the room. "If it was taken from outside, whoever it was wasn't mingling alongside Callie and Betsy. Which, you have to admit, settles the stomach a little."

"Go on."

"But, if it was taken outside, we don't have the luxury of narrowing down suspects by questioning everyone who was there. You know, the strange parent in the back of the room, or the person who didn't seem to go with anyone, or the guy who showed up for the cookies and milk but wasn't in the classroom during the kids' program."

He raked a hand through his hair in frustration. Tom was right. It was less likely a stranger would be noticed outside than inside.

"So what do we do?"

Glancing up, he took in the lieutenant's expression as the man responded to Tom's question. "We keep an eye on Miss Anderson. Make sure she's okay."

"Maybe she should go back to New York."

His partner's words made him freeze where he stood. "No! She's writing."

The right side of Tom's mouth slid upward. "She can write in New York, dude."

"She's writing here."

"You said she's your next-door neighbor, right?"

Kyle nodded at his lieutenant.

"And that you're involved, right?"

They were. Sort of. Or at least they were before he scared the bejeebers out of her. To his boss, though, he simply shrugged.

"Then keep an eye on her."

"Oh, he's already doing that, Lieutenant. Trust me on this."

He elbowed his partner in the gut. "That's not what he's saying."

"I know." Tom shrugged. "And, when you stop and think about it, chivalry could possibly trump chocolate, dude."

Suddenly it didn't matter whether Betsy could get past his being a cop. Did he want that? Of course.

But more than that, he wanted her safe.

Glancing from his boss to the photograph and back again, he felt a steely determination enveloping him from all sides. "They lay a hand on her and they will regret it."

"Let's just skip over the first part of that sentence, shall we?" Doug Grady lifted the picture from his desk and slipped it into a manila envelope. "Now get out of here. Both of you."

Following his partner's lead, Kyle stopped just outside the lieutenant's doorway and then turned around. "Hey, boss—thanks."

"Keep your eyes open, Brennan. And keep your girls safe."

His girls.

Callie and Betsy.

Hell would freeze over before he'd let harm come to either of them.

IT WAS NO USE. SHE SIMPLY couldn't write when she was upset. And she was upset. About Kyle.

She'd known from the beginning she should stay away. Yet she hadn't. She made him a picnic dinner.

She'd flirted with him while playing volleyball in his backyard. She'd let him kiss her. She fell for his daughter. And, like a fool, she'd fallen for him.

Hard.

Losing Mark in an instant had been hard, the images her mind had conjured regarding his death nothing short of torture. The guilt over their less than close relationship had merely been the icing on the cake.

But things were different now. She had feelings for Kyle—genuine feelings that were growing stronger with each passing day. If something happened to him…

Dropping onto the love seat in the sitting area off the front of the house, Betsy picked up the remote and aimed it at the television. The first few channels she came to offered daytime soaps followed by a smattering of game shows. Finally she stopped on a local midday news program.

Today's events included a story about a child in Cedar Creek who was found safe after wandering away from his home early that morning. A lucky cameraman, on hand to document the reunion between mother and child, provided the kind of visual footage that pulled at viewers' heartstrings—Betsy's included.

The second story involved the Cedar Creek Police Department and a rumored threat to one of its police officers. As Kyle's face emerged on the screen, Betsy sat up straight, her hand swiping at a stray tear from the previous story. According to the reporter who'd filed the report, rumors were swirling about Kyle's safety following the robbery at Linton Bank and Trust.

As the reporter spoke, it became obvious the story was constructed on limited details, none of which were being backed up by officials. But still, it would explain the presence of the home security company parked outside Kyle's home, the way his jaw tightened when she asked about the suspect at the school program, and the undeniable mood shift he'd displayed the night Callie called from her grandmother's house.

Was Kyle really in danger? And by extension, did that purported danger include Callie?

A shiver ran down her spine as she reached for the phone. Dialing Angela Murphy's number, she waited as ring after ring went unanswered. Finally, on the sixth ring, she picked up.

"Hello?"

"Angela—I mean, Ang? It's Betsy."

"Hi! Wow. Do you know that even after hanging out on your birthday, helping you look for a house and playing volleyball together in Kyle's backyard, I'm still having a hard time believing I actually know you?"

Surprised by the breathless excitement in Angela's voice, Betsy closed her eyes, willed herself to steer clear of the hurt that had landed her in front of the television in the first place. "I'm no different than you. I just write for a living."

"And entertain. And go out on tours. And sign books. And show up on morning news programs when each book comes out."

She let Angela's words wash over her, waiting for them to bring at least some small measure of a smile to her lips. But they didn't. Her mind, her thoughts, her concern were in one place and one place only.

"Did you see the news just now?"

"No. Why?"

The floodgates opened, words flowing from her mouth. "They said Kyle is in danger. Something to do with the bank robbery the other day." She heard the panic in her voice, felt a familiar fear building inside.

"Oh. That."

"So it's true?" she asked as she tightened her grip on the phone.

Several seconds elapsed before Angela responded. "It appears as if the guys they caught were members of a new gang. At best, they're a group of thugs with wounded egos. At worst, they're an actual gang, trying to get noticed by a bigger one. They were responsible for two other robberies before you arrived. Those, they got away with."

She felt her stomach flip-flop and she reached for a glass of water, the cool liquid doing little to dispel the sensation. Angela continued.

"Anyway, you were dead-on about the suspect and the camera that first night at the pizza place. Someone, who has been unwilling to step forward as yet, tipped off the department to the fact that some very real nonverbal communication was going on in that picture—a rally cry for retribution."

"And since Kyle is the officer standing next to him in that shot, he's become the target of that rally cry?"

"It looks that way."

She inhaled slowly, her mind trying desperately to process everything she was hearing. "Is that why Callie has been spending so much time at her grandmother's?"

"Yes."

Lifting the curtain beside the couch, she peered outside for the umpteenth time that morning. "Is that why there's a home security truck parked outside Kyle's house right now?"

"Yes."

Her instincts had been right. Kyle was in danger. Real danger.

"Betsy? Are you okay?"

It was just as her head had been trying to warn her heart from the beginning. Police officers, like firefighters, didn't have safe jobs. Fires killed. And criminals looking for payback killed, too.

It was a fact.

"Betsy?"

Mark's death had robbed him of a life he loved. And it had robbed them of a chance to find out whether they could turn their marriage around.

His death had also sent her spiraling into a depression that had affected every aspect of her life for nearly a year. A depression she was just now beginning to shed. Did she really want to go back to a life like that? Could she?

"I can't do this," she whispered.

"Do what?"

"Um…"

"Do what?" Angela repeated. "C'mon…tell me."

She was unable to hold her fears in any longer. "Travel this road again. It nearly destroyed me the first time. Mark said he could handle things, too. But he got trapped in a fire anyway. And now there's Kyle."

Silence filled her ear for a moment. Finally, Angela spoke, her words small comfort against a reality she knew all too well. "I read about your husband and I'm sorry. It was a tragic, horrible accident. But those happen every day, Betsy. Whether you're a firefighter or a police officer or some person simply standing in the wrong place at the wrong time. You can't walk away from the good things in life simply because of what *might* happen. He'll be okay, Betsy. Kyle is a smart guy. Tom says he's working this case during all hours of the night…tracking leads, talking to people, piecing the identity of this gang together little by little. He'll have them rounded up in no time."

"And if he doesn't?"

"You can't let ifs rule your life, Betsy."

It was a sentiment she'd heard before. "Look, I better go. I have to get back to the computer." She stood, her eyes riveted on the paneled truck next door. "My editor wanted this book a zillion yesterdays ago."

She knew she was being dismissive cutting their conversation short this way, but she couldn't help it…

It was time for her heart to stop calling the shots.

Chapter Eleven

Kyle sat in his car, staring at Betsy's house. He'd been so hopeful his partner's suggestion of chocolate would be enough to smooth away any brusqueness he may have exuded the last time he saw her. But now, after Tom's call, he wasn't so sure.

Chocolate was okay for things like a snippy tone or a bout of miscommunication, but it didn't stand a chance against fear.

And Betsy was scared.

He got that. Heck, he was scared, too. Hurt came in different packages. And, for whatever reason, they were being thrust into a situation that had an uneasy pang of familiarity for both of them.

Betsy was a celebrity in her own right. Yet, she wasn't Lila. Not from what he'd seen so far, anyway.

He was a police officer facing a potentially dangerous situation like Betsy's late husband. Only he wasn't Mark. Sure, he took his job seriously. But it didn't define him and it never would. Fatherhood did that.

Somehow, someway, he needed to convince Betsy of that while apologizing for his own missteps. Unfortunately, based on the heads-up he'd just gotten from Tom, the convincing part was going to be the hardest.

He swung his gaze toward the white paneled truck outside his home, the security company's logo a nice warning to anyone scoping the neighborhood. He'd really thought he was getting close. The family ties between the two bank robbers had been tricky to trace but he'd accomplished it nonetheless. And thanks to a few sources who'd been willing to talk to him at one of the local bars earlier in the week, the suspects had kin in a few neighboring counties—all of whom had criminal records.

Slowly but surely he'd been piecing together the members of the family, discarding those who seemed unlikely to be part of a gang. But time was no longer a luxury. The notion they might have him in their crosshairs was now a reality.

Maybe Tom had been right. Maybe Betsy *should* go back to New York to finish her book. Maybe it truly was the safest way to go.

Only problem was, he wanted her here.

Squaring his shoulders, he opened the driver's side door and stepped onto the road, his focus firmly planted on Betsy's front door. Propelled forward by her image, he bypassed his own home in favor of hers, turning back only to retrieve the box of chocolates Tom had convinced him to buy earlier in the day.

When he finally reached her front porch, he held the ribbon-wrapped package behind his back and rang the bell with the other, the sound wafting through the windows on either side of the door. Footsteps followed as did a stirring in his chest at the sight of Betsy walking toward him in a pair of body-hugging white shorts and a tropical blue T-shirt.

Resisting the urge to yank the door open and pull her into his arms, he simply smiled, an expression he realized she did not mirror—with her mouth or her eyes. His heart sank.

"Kyle."

"Hi, Betsy. How are you today?" He knew the words were forced, stilted even, but he was suddenly tongue-tied, his resolve weakened by her demeanor.

"Fine. Busy."

"Are you writing?"

"Trying to."

He winced at her aloofness, willed himself to concentrate on the task at hand. "That's good. Look, I wanted to stop by for several reasons."

She waited, the screen door still separating them.

"First, an apology. I'm sorry I was so evasive yesterday. I guess I'm not used to having someone to talk to about work. I've been single for a long time. And it never dawned on me that by leaving you in the dark, I may have been causing you unneeded stress."

"I'm not sure telling me every single detail would make a difference."

He held his palm up against the screen. "I'm going to be okay, Betsy."

"That's what Mark always said."

"But I'm not Mark. I've never made the job the focus of my every waking minute. I have Callie for that. And knowing she's counting on me is all the reminder I need to play it smart. She needs a father, not a cowboy, Betsy."

Her shoulders relaxed slightly, a sign he took to keep going.

"Which brings me to the second thing—a thank-you. For doing Callie's hair...for coming to the reading...for encouraging her to write that unforgettable poem that I will treasure for the rest of my life."

"She told you about that?"

"Yeah, she did. She told me she wrote it all, but that it was your idea to put her feelings for me onto paper."

Betsy shrugged, a noncommittal gesture probably designed to mask the thawing in her eyes. But he saw it anyway.

Buoyed by the possibility he was making headway, he continued. "And because Tom seems to know more about women than I do, I brought you a present." He pulled the box from behind his back and held it toward the screen door.

When she said nothing, he rushed to speak, his words sounding silly even to his own ears. "If this isn't your equivalent to a guy's beer gene, I apologize. But he insisted it was and I remembered how much you seemed to enjoy the brownies the other night at our picnic and—"

"Beer gene?"

"Yeah. Tom says all women like chocolate as a peace offering. That it's in your genes. Like beer is for most guys."

She laughed, a sound he welcomed in more ways than one.

"So? Was he right?"

"About the chocolate? Or the peace offering part?"

"Both, I guess."

"I want him to be right, Kyle, I really do. It's just that…well, I'm scared."

"So am I."

The reappearance of fear on her face made him rush to explain. "I'm feeling things for you I vowed I wouldn't let myself feel again. And, like you, there's a measure of fear that comes with not knowing whether I might be wrong about you."

She studied him for a long moment, a visual inspection he welcomed as a sign of progress. What, exactly, she was thinking, he didn't know. But at least she was finally looking at him.

Baby steps.

Jutting her chin in the direction of his house she finally spoke, her tone tinged with an undeniable pinch of worry. "So what's with the security system?"

He pondered the various things he could say, techniques to soften the blow, but he opted, instead, for the truth. It was the only way.

"There's a chance I've pissed off some people. And there's a chance they might want to exact a little retribution." He shifted foot to foot. "So...we're taking a few precautions."

"Like a security system to protect Callie?"

"Yes. Though she's staying with my mom right now. I feel better knowing she's there."

She pointed at the bulge under his shirt. "Like carrying your weapon home from work?"

"Yes. And like asking you to keep your doors and windows locked and to call me the second you hear anything unusual."

Her eyes widened as her mouth gaped open.

"A picture showed up at work today."

"A picture?"

He nodded. "Of you."

"I don't understand."

"Whoever these guys are, they've tied you to me." He raked a hand through his hair with a renewed sense of frustration. "There's a chance they're just blowing smoke. Trying to freak me out. But there's a chance they're not. And that's enough of a chance for me."

He waited, giving her time to process everything

he'd thrown at her. When she finally spoke, he hung on every word. "I need to know you're taking care of *you*. I don't want you distracted by some phantom threat to me. Maybe I should just go back to New York."

"No! Please. Give me a chance to do my job and look out for you."

"Look out for me?" she asked as she peered up at him through thick lashes.

"While I'm at work, maybe you could take your laptop to the library or the coffee shop and write there."

"Okay…"

"And once I'm home, where I can keep an eye on things, you could come back."

"But won't you want to be at your mom's? Spending time with Callie?"

He shook his head. "Not if it means leading them to her. No, I need to stay here…where I can be sure you're okay, too."

She pushed open the screen door and stepped onto the porch. "I'll be okay if I know you are, too."

He stared at her in awe, her concern for him reaching deep inside his soul. Betsy Anderson was a keeper. Of that, there was no doubt.

How to make her *his* keeper, though, was anyone's guess.

"IF YOU'D FEEL SAFER, you could stay here," he said as he led her down the hallway and into the spare room beside Callie's. "It's nothing fancy but it would be adequate. And you could write here during the day now that I have the alarm system."

She peeked over his shoulder at the full-size bed neatly covered with a colonial-style spread, her thoughts traveling to places she knew they shouldn't. Kyle was worried about her safety and nothing more.

And she was terrified for his.

"I'm sure I'll be fine in my own home," she said, her voice suddenly raspy. "I'm a big girl, you know."

"I just don't know what these guys are up to yet. They've established the fact that we were at Callie's reading together. And while I'd like to assume they'd target me directly, I just can't be sure."

"I just want them to go away…move on to another town somewhere else."

"And if they do, they'll just be a danger to someone else. No, this needs to be stopped. Here." He leaned against the east wall of the room, his gaze lingering on the bed for a moment before reengaging hers. "You sure I can't talk you into staying with me?"

She shook her head. "The eye stuff and the baseball bat will be fine."

"Okay." He pulled open the top dresser drawer and extracted a can of pepper spray. "You spray it in an intruder's eyes just the way I said and—" he shut the drawer and reached behind the bed "—then you hit him with this baseball bat for good measure."

"For good measure," she repeated as she sat down on the edge of the bed then dropped across it like a rag doll. "And what do you have?"

"What do you mean?"

"To protect yourself?"

"My gun for starters."

Grabbing a pillow from the head of the bed, Betsy hugged it against her chest, Kyle's answer bringing a lump to her throat that made talking difficult. Instead, she simply nodded, hoped the response would be enough to ward off a potentially painful conversation.

It didn't work. He persisted. "You're *that* worried about me right now?"

"I have been since that first day."

A huskiness overtook his voice as his finger trailed down her chin and along the side of her neck. "You worry about people a lot, huh?"

"Not really, no. But I do…about you." She closed her eyes as his finger left the nape of her neck, the heat from his skin making her long for more. When his fingers stopped just shy of her breasts, she opened her eyes, peered at him through tear-dappled lashes. "I want you to be safe. For Callie."

"For Callie?" he repeated.

"Y-yes."

Anchoring his hands beneath her arms, he scooted her upward until the upper half of her body was cradled in his arms. "Because I'm getting a sense there's something else going on here."

She swallowed. "Something else?"

"Yeah. Like this…" He leaned forward, his mouth coming down on hers. With a burst of intensity he slipped his tongue between her lips, reveled in the moan of desire that ensued.

As the kiss grew even deeper, his hands began to roam, his fingers following the same path they'd forged earlier, this time failing to stop at the same place. As he reached the curve of her breast, he pulled back. "Am I warm?"

"Warm?"

"Yeah…am I getting closer to figuring out what else is going on here?"

"I—" She stopped as his mouth trailed his fingers down her neck. When his mouth reached the swell of her breast, his hand moved ahead to the buttons on her shirt. As the fabric fell from her body, he pulled back once again, the appreciation in his eyes bringing a shiver down her spine.

With a practiced hand, he unhooked her bra. She squirmed with pleasure as he brought his mouth to her breast, teasing her nipple with his tongue. Slowly, deliberately, she arched her back, her breast jutting forward against his mouth. He sucked harder, intensifying her moan tenfold.

And then he stopped, his body tensing as he bolted upright on the bed, the pace of their breathing no longer in sync.

"What's wrong?" she whispered as her fingers threaded through his hair and tried to bring his mouth down to her body once again.

"Shh." With one finger to his lips, Kyle slid out from underneath her, rising from the bed and disappearing into the hallway with the stealth of a cat.

She strained to pick out a sound of any kind as his shadow grew smaller, his footsteps nearly impossible to detect.

A vaguely familiar yet entirely different fear gripped her heart as she, too, scooted off the bed, her hands finding the buttons of her shirt and securing them once again. For what seemed like the ten most magical minutes of her life, Betsy had finally gotten a glimpse of what passion truly meant. Never, during her engagement or relatively short marriage to Mark, had she ever felt the way Kyle made her feel.

His touch electrified her, made her feel wanted and needed and, even, sexy. But as wonderful as it was to feel needed by someone else, she had absolutely no intention of ever letting herself feel that way for someone else.

Need spawned weakness. She knew that, believed it with every ounce of her being.

Life was unpredictable enough on its own. Why on earth would she willingly choose to fall head over heels in love with someone who could be ripped from her life at any moment? Living through tragedy was hard enough. Living through tragedy with a shattered heart was simply unfathomable.

She started down the hallway, her decision solidifying with each step she took, Kyle's lean, strong form coming into view once again as she rounded the corner into the family room. He turned and looked at her, his tall body nothing more than a shadow against the brightness of an exterior light that had been tripped by some sort of motion.

"Is everything okay?"

Shrugging, he turned back to the window, his voice tense. "Someone was outside the house. But by the time I got in here, he was running down the road and jumping on a bike." He raked a hand through his hair then let it fall at his side in a tight fist. "I called the department but it's unlikely they'll find him. There's six different ways to get out of this area once you leave this street and even though he was on a motorcycle there's still no guarantee they'll locate him."

"I'm sorry." She heard the shake in her words despite their quiet tone.

"So am I." His back still to her, he continued to peer outside. "I simply didn't move fast enough."

She tried again. "No, I mean…I'm sorry…but I have to leave."

He looked over his shoulder at her, his facial features easier to identify in the absence of light from the motion sensor. "I'll go with you."

She shifted from foot to foot, her gaze skirting the floor, the couch and the knickknack-covered mantel before finally meeting his once again. "No. I'll take the spray and the bat. That's enough."

His jaw dropped as he turned all the way around. "Don't you get it? Someone was just outside my home. Someone who's linked us together."

Inhaling deeply, she mustered the courage she needed to stand her ground despite Kyle's disagreement. "So they have a picture of me, big deal. That doesn't mean they know where I live. My name is not listed in a phone book or on a deed recorded in any local government office. I'm fine on my own."

"You're fine on your own, huh?" he repeated, his eyes narrowed on her face.

"It's my preference, actually."

"Your pref—so that's it? You can just walk out the door without so much as a care in the world as to my feelings?" He flung his hands in the air, his mouth forming an angry slit across his face. "Wow. And here I thought you were different."

"Different? Different than what?"

"Not *what*, Betsy. *Whom*."

"I don't under—" She stopped, the meaning of his words hitting like a slap across the face. "Wait. You tell me you're not like Mark. Yet you don't think twice about making me one and the same with your ex-wife?"

"You are female, aren't you?"

She stopped at the door, the cruelty of his words raining down on her as she considered her reply. Should she reiterate her fear? Should she tell him that watching him leave for work or run outside at every sound was a pain she simply couldn't handle? Should she tell him she was terrified at the notion of losing him one day?

No.

Not now. Not with the things he'd said. Sometimes the lie was better, easier. On everyone. And if it accomplished the same thing, what difference did it really make?

Squaring her shoulders she turned to face him one last time, her throat tight with disappointment, her heart heavy with sadness. "Yeah, that's it, Kyle. I'm a selfish person. My number one concern at all times is myself and my own needs."

Chapter Twelve

If she'd realized anger was such a powerful writing tool, she'd have sought it out months earlier rather than letting some bookstore calendar uproot her from her life and drag her halfway across the country to accomplish the same thing. Still, scrolling her way through her work in progress, she couldn't help but feel encouraged regardless of the match that struck the flame.

She'd been too keyed up to sleep when she returned from Kyle's, his accusations making short work of any lingering sadness and morphing it into the emotion that had helped her crank out ten pages during the night. Ten pages that brought her further into the book and closer to meeting her deadline.

With a double click on Save, Betsy rose from her chair and stood at the sunporch window that afforded the best view of her neighbor's home across the hedge line. She'd heard him leave for work nearly two hours earlier, the sound of his car making her type faster.

Kyle Brennan was a jerk. A first-class jerk.

Shaking her head at the memory of his pompous accusation, she wandered into the kitchen and over to the stove. Coffee was her morning staple. It was the one thing she could count on each day to get her up and moving. Today was no exception. Even though she'd gotten in a good day's work already, sleep wasn't something she could indulge in just yet. When she hit twenty-five pages, maybe…

Who did he think he was, likening her to a woman who cared about no one but herself?

She turned the handle on the front right burner, the sound of the gas igniter lost against the angry questions firing through her mind…

Did she not walk away from her writing to help Callie get ready for her program? Did Callie not tell him about the poem she'd encouraged the little girl to write? Had she not volunteered to keep Callie with her while Kyle was at work? Had she not admitted to him she was scared for his safety?

As the water heated, she grabbed a coffee mug from the cabinet and clunked it down on the counter, her free hand instinctively reaching for the tin of coffee and pulling it close.

To have Kyle insinuate she was selfish was simply too much. It was wrong and it was unfair.

Or was it?

When the water was ready she poured it into her mug, watching the steam rise in swirls. Did she plant herself on his front step about the time he was due home from work? Did she set him straight on who she was and who she wasn't?

No. Because even if she came clean as to the reason she left, the big picture wouldn't change.

She could handle the heartache of walking away on her own two feet. Sure, it was painful. She had real feelings for this man. Feelings that were both foreign and wonderful all at the same time. But what she couldn't handle was having him ripped from her life without warning.

Especially when he'd take her heart with her.

Lacing her fingers through the handle, Betsy pulled the mug to her chest and closed her eyes. Maybe staying in Cedar Creek wasn't such a good idea. She'd already gotten the jump she needed to get writing. The words were flowing. So why stay?

Because you signed a three-month lease.

Hindsight was always twenty-twenty. She knew that better than anyone. But knowing it and learning from it were two separate things.

Besides, the hassle of moving back would only slow her progress on the book. And she liked it here. She liked the people she'd met at the school, she liked having her own yard, and she liked the pace that was Cedar Creek. Not too fast and never impatient.

On second thought, Cedar Creek was the perfect place to finish the book. It just happened to have one pitfall.

Kyle Brennan.

"BACK IT UP A LITTLE MORE."

He glanced at his partner in the passenger seat, his daydreaming stymied by the man's instructions. "What?"

"Back it up a little more." Tom pointed out the front windshield. "The weather dude said it's gonna be a near-scorcher today and I'd rather spend the next hour sitting in shade than baking in the sun."

"Okay." He slipped the gearshift into Reverse and backed their patrol car farther into a grove of maple trees. The spot, itself, was just off a dirt road on the northern edge of town—the kind of place few people frequented unless they had a reason.

Like being up to no good.

"So tell me again what this guy in the coffeehouse said?"

Kyle slid the car into Park, lowered their windows and leaned back against the seat, his focus squarely on the road in front of them. "He said he'd heard talk about a gang. A group of cousins hell-bent on bucking the law."

Tom hooked his left leg at the knee and turned to face Kyle. "I wish the lieutenant would give us five minutes alone with those scumbags from the bank. Five minutes to get what we need from them."

"I wouldn't be opposed to that." He stared out the front windshield. "But, since we know that can't happen, I'm going other routes. Like this guy at the coffeehouse."

Tom nodded. "If this band of thugs are truly cousins, shouldn't that make it easier for us to track them down? Can't we get some genealogist in to help us trace the bank perps' family tree?"

"They're not really related. Something about ties through various marriages and life essentially throwing them together."

"Ahh. That kind of stuff makes my head hurt. Just give me a flowchart with boxes to follow and I'm okay." Tom pointed toward the road they had under surveillance. "And why are we here again?"

"My source said there's been increased bike traffic out here lately. And, since our perps were riding bikes when they tried to hit up the bank, I just think it needs to be checked out."

"The guy last night…he was on a bike, right?"

Kyle nodded, his teeth clenched.

"Did you get a look at him at all?"

"No," he snapped. "By the time I got into the living room, he was disappearing down the road."

"Was he alone?"

"It's possible there was someone else. I didn't even realize he was on a motorcycle until a few minutes later when I heard the roar. He must have parked it down a house or two."

"And since this dude at the coffee shop mentioned increased bike traffic out this way, you want to see if the two go hand in hand?"

He shot a look at his friend. "Wouldn't you?"

"Whoa, dude. I'm not second-guessing you. Just getting myself up to speed." Tom pushed back against the passenger side door and stared at Kyle. "There's something else going on with you this morning."

"You mean, beyond the fact that I've got some dirtbag skulking around my house because I apprehended his buddy?" Kyle waved a dismissive hand in the air. "Nah, that about covers it."

"It's Betsy, isn't it?"

"No!"

Tom laughed. "You're such a lousy liar."

He turned his head, focused his gaze outside the driver's side window in an attempt to regain the composure he knew he was losing.

"She didn't like the idea of you hovering over her under the guise of protecting her, huh?"

In an instant he was back in the spare bedroom of his home, Betsy in his arms, his hands exploring the lusciousness of her body. He clamped his mouth shut to stifle the memory-worthy groan. "She seemed okay with it. At first. Heck, things were even getting hot and heavy."

"Hot and heavy?"

The intrigue in Tom's voice made him laugh in spite of himself. "Hot and heavy."

"Details?"

The smile left his lips. "The details are simple. Things felt awesome and then she walked. Said she preferred to be on her own. And she wasn't just talking about protection when she said that. She was talking about me."

"That doesn't sound like Betsy." Tom dropped his left foot onto the floor mat and repositioned himself in the vinyl seat. "She's not like that."

"And how the hell do you know?" Kyle spat. "You sit across from her at a pizza parlor for a few hours one night, lose your shorts to us in a volleyball game one evening and that makes you an expert on Betsy Anderson?"

For a moment there was only silence in the car, the anger in Kyle's words hovering in the air. When Tom finally spoke, his normal genial tone was gone, in its place a cocktail of disappointment and distaste. "You should hear yourself, Kyle. I mean, really hear yourself. You are still so disgustingly bitter over Lila's leaving that—"

"This has nothing to do with Lila," he snapped.

"Oh, no? Are you sure? Did you ask Betsy why she split?"

Had he? He wasn't sure.

"Or did you start hurling accusations?"

Kyle smacked the heel of his hand against the steering wheel as his partner continued, the man's words more truthful than he realized. "News flash, dude...you made a bad choice when you hooked up with your ex. That's it. It happens to everyone at some point. What matters is how you rebound."

"I've rebounded."

"No, you haven't. You're still carrying the same chip on your shoulder you've had since Lila left. But here's something to chew on for a minute—Betsy isn't Lila. Never was. Isn't. And sure as hell never will be."

He stared at his friend. "Then why did she go from being putty in my hands to walking out my door?"

"I suspect the reason can be found in the in-between part."

"The in-between part?"

Tom nodded. "Did something happen between the make-out fest and her leaving?"

He snorted. "Yeah, the loser casing my house showed up on my property and pulled the focus off of her."

"Did she know something was wrong?"

"I'm sure the fact that I left her without notice and ran down the hall was some indication." Pulling his attention from his partner, he fastened it on the dirt road once again.

"Do you think—I don't know. Maybe, just maybe, she was scared?"

"Scared?"

"Yeah...scared."

"What? That I couldn't keep her safe?" He threw his hands into the air in frustration.

"I was thinking more along the lines of her being scared that something would happen to you?"

Suddenly it was all crystal clear—the fear in her eyes when she came around the corner, the slump of her shoulders when she saw him standing by the window.

Betsy hadn't been upset because he'd run out on her. She'd been worried. Terrified, even.

He was an idiot. A first-class idiot.

Chapter Thirteen

She sat in the exact same spot she'd sat the first day, a blanket spread beneath her. Only this time, instead of sitting untouched in its bag, her computer was alive and well, smack-dab in the middle of her lap.

The words were flowing for the second time that day, only instead of being propelled by anger, they were being spawned by a different emotion.

Sadness.

Try as she might to get Kyle out of her mind, she couldn't. And try as she might to concentrate on the cruelty of his words, she couldn't dismiss the reason they were there.

Experience.

She wished she could be angry that he was holding her feet to a fire of someone else's making, but she couldn't. Because, in a sense, she was doing the same thing to him—shying away from her feelings for fear of a tragedy that someone else befell.

In quiet moments like now, with Paxton Bridge as her writing backdrop, it all made sense. The peace that emanated from the stone structure and its parklike surroundings helped her to see clearly. But when she was alone in her head with her memories, or acutely aware of her heart as she was whenever Kyle was around, fear took over, dictating her words and ruling her actions.

It had to stop.

With her fingers poised above the keyboard, she looked up, marveled at the way the afternoon sun lent a magical aura to the stones that arched across the small, picturesque lake. There was no denying it. Something about Paxton Bridge calmed her soul, allowed her to consider things from a different perspective, finding hope in the process.

Whether Kyle Brennan was worth pursuing was a mystery. They both came with baggage that affected the way they saw each other. Whether it was baggage they could discard before they ruined the undeniable spark between them was anyone's guess.

But question mark or not, it was something that had to be done. For herself.

If nothing else, her time with Kyle was proof she didn't want to spend her life alone. Not if there was someone out there who could make her feel. Really, truly *feel*. She'd missed out on that with Mark. And he'd missed out on that with her.

She swallowed over the lump that rose in her throat at the realization. It had been so easy to dwell on the fact that she'd felt empty every time her husband had walked out the door to hang with his friends at the firehouse rather than spend time together. But Mark must have felt it, too. If he hadn't, he wouldn't have left as often as he did. It was a freeing thought, a revelation that removed some of the guilt she'd carried for far too long.

Sliding her laptop to the grass, she pulled her knees to her chest and rested her chin on them. As silly as it was to admit, she owed Paxton Bridge more than a little gratitude. Somehow, someway, its gentle arch had provided her first glimmer of hope in entirely too long. The hope, in turn, had freed her mind of the weight that had prevented her from writing. The decision to stay in Cedar Creek while she worked on her next book had enabled her to meet Kyle.

And Callie.

Her lips spread upward at the mere thought of the little girl, a child so happy and so sweet that it was impossible not to love her. She was a tribute to her father whether he realized it or not. Children like Callie didn't just fall from trees. They were nurtured and loved and taught right from—

"Miss Anderson? Is that you?"

Betsy lifted her head and turned toward the voice, her smile growing ever wider at the sight of her latest round of woolgathering. "Hi, Callie, isn't this a wonderful surprise!" Peeking around the little girl, she scanned the immediate vicinity for Kyle but to no avail. She looked back at Callie. "Where's your dad?"

"He's working. I had a half day today so my grandma brought me here to play." Callie pointed at Betsy's laptop. "Are you writing?"

She glanced at the computer and nodded. "I was. But I guess I just needed a break."

"What kind of break?"

"A thinking break mostly."

"I take those sometimes, too." Callie cocked her head to the left and studied Betsy closely. "Whatcha thinking about?"

"Lots of things, I guess. My book, that bridge—" she gestured toward the Paxton "—and you."

"Me? Really?"

She couldn't help but laugh at the excitement in the child's face. "Yes, you. I was thinking about how sweet you are and how lucky your daddy is to have a daughter like you."

The little girl beamed. "My grandma is back there—" she said, pointing over her shoulder, "talking to Mrs. Walters. But she said I could go down by the bridge and see if there are any frogs hopping around. Wanna come?"

"Frogs?"

"Uh-huh! Big ones!"

"Big ones?"

Callie nodded, her smile nearly splitting her face in two. "So…do you?"

"I—I…well, I guess. If you want." Betsy looked from her computer to the bridge and back again. "But I'll need to keep an eye on my computer while we're down there, okay?"

"Okay." Reaching her small hand outward, Callie took hold of Betsy's arm and fairly tugged her to her feet. "C'mon, let's go!"

Caught up in the child's excitement, Betsy followed Kyle's daughter down to the kidney-shaped lake, Paxton Bridge spanning the narrow-most part of the water. As they neared the base of the bridge, Callie pointed, her small index finger guiding Betsy's attention to a series of black marks just inside the water-side of the footbridge. "Is that gaffidy?"

"Gaffidy?"

"That stuff people paint when they're not s'posed to?"

Her head snapped up. "Oh…you mean, graffiti." She took hold of Callie's hand as they drew closer. "It sure looks that way."

"Daddy's not gonna be happy. He says people need to paint on paper like I do."

With each step forward, the markings transformed into letters and the letters came together to form words....

"Look, Miss Anderson! It says Brennan...just like my last name!" Callie lurched forward with excitement, her tiny hand nearly slipping from Betsy's grasp as she tried to run closer.

Instinctively, Betsy tightened her grip, pulled the child close as her own gaze focused on the words that stretched their way along the interior arch.

Brennan Will Pay.

She heard the gasp as it escaped her mouth, felt the child still beside her. "What's wrong, Miss Anderson?"

Like a moth to a flame, she read the words again... and again...and again.

Brennan Will Pay.

"What's that mean, Miss Anderson?"

Realizing the child was reading along with her, she turned on her heels and headed back toward the blanket, Callie's hand firmly in her grasp. "I think they forgot a few letters. That's all."

"Like what?"

The child was nothing if not persistent. First the cookies, now the graffiti.

"For starters...an *L* for *play*." She cast a sidelong glance in Callie's direction as they walked, hoped her attempt at diversion worked.

"Brennan will play?" Callie asked.

"And I think it was supposed to say Shannon...not Brennan."

"Hey! I know a Shannon. She's in my class at school. And she really, really likes to play." Skipping along on the grass beside her, Callie kept on chattering, her voice mingling with the white noise in Betsy's head.

She had to tell Kyle. Had to warn him. But not now, not with his daughter in the park.

"Could you do me a favor?" She stopped at the base of her blanket and swung Callie to a stop in front of her.

"Okay."

"Could you go find your grandma? I just realized I have a really important call to make and I don't like the idea of you playing by the lake with no one watching."

"But what about the frogs?" Callie protested.

"Uh...how about we save that for another day? We can even make a whole day of it. First frogs, then shopping. And then, if you're really good, we'll even get ice cream." Slipping her hand inside her pocket, she pulled out her cell phone and flipped it open. "What do you say? Will that work?"

"Well—hey! There's Peter!" Callie pointed toward the playground not far from where her grandmother stood talking to another gray-haired woman. "Peter is in my class."

She sent up a silent prayer of thanks. "Then you go on and play. We'll do frogs next—"

In a flash, the little girl was gone, her strawberry-blond ponytail bouncing against her neck as she ran toward the playground. For the briefest of moments, Betsy simply stood there and watched, her heart completely captivated by the ball of energy that was Callie Brennan.

A ball of energy that needed to be protected at all costs....

IT WAS NEARLY NINE O'CLOCK when he knocked. The family room was shadowed in a darkness peppered only by the candlelight scattered about. She'd lit the candles in an attempt to calm her nerves, to bring a sense of peace where there was none.

The rational side of her mind told her he was fine, that the graffiti sighting she'd called in had simply kept him busy. The other side—the part that always made things worse—told her the call had led to a showdown with the perpetrators and that he had been hurt.

Silly, really, but there it was.

She closed her eyes with relief as he knocked again, the staccato sound a welcome reprieve from an evening spent watching and worrying. If she had a dime for every time she'd jumped from the couch when a car slowed on the street, she'd have no need to write. Yet if she'd had to return said dimes for every time it hadn't been Kyle, she'd be right where she was, pounding the keyboard morning, noon and night.

But he was finally here—alive and well and standing on her front porch. Knocking.

And waiting.

"Betsy? Are you there?"

For her...

Jumping from her sentry post on the love seat, Betsy nearly ran to the screen door. As she drew closer, her feet slowed despite the opposite effect on her heart.

Kyle Brennan was gorgeous. There was no getting around that fact. She'd known it since day one. Yet it seemed as if the stress he was under not only increased his appeal but jettisoned it into a smoldering hotness that brought a flush to her face and a tingle to places that hadn't tingled in a very long time. His eyes were still breathtakingly blue, but now, with everything going on, they held a steely determination that she found arousing. Especially when they were trained on her.

She stopped just inside the door and swallowed. "Hi."

It was a pathetic greeting and she knew it. But it was all she could think to say against the pounding of her heart.

"Hi, yourself." His gaze flickered across her face before slipping slowly down, the appreciation in his expression impossible to miss.

She swallowed again. "Hi."

He laughed, the sound so real, so rich she couldn't help but crack a smile, as well. "You already said that."

"And I can say it again, too… Hi." Unable to hold back the questions any longer, words began to pour from her mouth, the intensity enough to make a person's head spin. Including her own. "Are you okay? Did Angela tell you? Were there any problems?"

Smacking his left forearm with his right hand once and then twice, he raised an eyebrow skyward. "I can— and want to—answer every single one of those questions, I really do. But is there any chance I could come inside? The bugs out here seem fairly determined to have me for dessert."

"They're not the only ones," she muttered under her breath as she wrapped her fingers around the handle and pushed. Realizing she'd shared one of her fantasies aloud, she coughed and tried again. "I'm sorry…come on in."

She sucked in her breath as he stepped into the house, his hip grazing hers as he passed. "Would you like something to drink?"

His voice was husky as he stopped beside her. Leaning

forward, he cupped her face in his hands. "There's a lot of things I want right now. Things I want to say. Things I want to do. Having a drink is definitely not one of them."

She searched his sapphire-blue eyes for something to discount the meaning she was deciphering from his words, but there was nothing. Nothing except the same raw desire that was making her hands moisten and her mouth grow dry.

"You are beautiful, do you know that?" His words echoed in her ears as he brought his lips to her forehead and held them against her skin, his breath warm and exciting and oh so very sexy.

"I…"

"C'mon, let's sit." Stepping back, he dropped his hands from her face, his right seeking the small of her back instead and guiding her toward the family room. When they reached the doorway, he stopped. "Candles?"

"I needed them." It was all she could think to say. The memory of his breath on her skin had short-circuited any ability she had for intelligent speech.

For a moment there was only silence as she felt his gaze roaming over her body once again, a visual inspection she not only enjoyed but welcomed, as well. "I know something about need."

She looked up, felt her knees weaken at the sight of the naked longing in his eyes. Suddenly nervous, she rushed to explain, to counteract the sexually charged atmosphere with something a bit less heavy. Yes, she wanted Kyle. *Needed* him, even, if the yearning in her body was to be believed. But it was the need she felt growing in her heart that frightened her most.

"I was worried. I tried watching some TV, but that

didn't work. I just kept flipping the channel back to news and dreading what they might say." She glanced down at the floor, her bare feet barely visible in the glow from the candlelight. "I tried reading, but I'd get to the end of a chapter and realize I hadn't absorbed a thing. I tried writing, but that was no use, either."

His hand inched up her back until it was at the base of her neck. "So what did you do?"

She met his eyes with her own as she turned toward him. "I lit the candles to calm my nerves and I listened."

"Listened for what?"

"You," she whispered as he pulled her to him, his mouth closing down on hers with an intensity that made her gasp. She snaked her arms around his neck as the kiss deepened, his own hand moving upward to play with her hair—to tip her head ever so gently as his lips left hers in search of her chin, her neck, her shoulders.

She groaned with pleasure as his free hand reached up to the back of her neck once again. With two quick tugs, he pulled the ties of her shirt free to reveal the skimpy pink strapless bra underneath. Slowly yet deliberately, he bowed his head still farther, his lips finding the top of her breasts and leaving a trail of kisses that left her breathless.

Nothing could have prepared her for this moment, for the feeling of pure desire that pulsed throughout her body at the feel of his mouth on her skin. He felt it, too. Of that she was certain.

Pulling back ever so slightly, she peered up at him, his erection pushing against her leg. "I want you, Kyle Brennan."

The second the words left her lips, his hand traveled around to her back once again, this time to unhook her bra and let it fall to her feet. He moaned with pleasure as he drank in her body with his eyes before seeking her breasts with his hands.

She dug her fingers into his muscled back as he replaced his hands with his mouth, his tongue teasing her nipples as they hardened with desire.

"Look," he instructed, his voice heavy with need. "Look at us on the wall."

She willed her mind to focus on his words, to do as he asked. But it was hard. The sensation of his mouth on her breasts had left her void of everything except a desire to beg for more.

"Look."

Slowly, she opened her eyes, her longing intensifying even more as she focused on their candlelit shadows intertwined on the wall. His toned body moved back just enough to create a separation then dropped to the ground as his hands sought the buttons of her jeans.

Still watching their shadows, she ran her fingers through his hair as he slid her jeans off her hips and down her legs. When they pooled at her feet, she stepped out, her skin tingling at the feel of his lips as they traveled from her knees to her thighs, his fingers moving her thong to the side to allow access to her heat.

A groan escaped her lips as she pulled her focus from the wall, her eyes rolling back in her head as Kyle's tongue brought her to the edge and then over. Slowly, he repositioned her thong only to slide the entire thing down her legs as he looked up, his gaze locked with hers.

As she stepped out of her panties, he stood, the fire in his eyes propelling her to slide her hands under his shirt and lift it over his head, the tautness of his muscles heightening her desire still more. Reaching down, she undid his pants, her body craning toward his with an overpowering need to know him in the most intimate of ways.

Without breaking eye contact, he lifted his pants from the floor, removing a foil wrapper from his front pocket. Wordlessly, she nodded, her eyes never leaving his as she lowered herself to the floor, her hand tugging him downward to join her. With her eyes fixed on his, she wrapped her hand around him and guided him inside her, their bodies joining together with a thrust that made them both scream out with pleasure. She looked from the wall to him and back again, the sensation of his length moving inside her matched only by the image of his body lifting and falling over hers as their breath became one.

Time after time he brought her to the brink only to slow things down, his willpower maddeningly wonderful. Each thrust of his body sent her head spinning as she cried out for more— a more he accommodated again and again until he couldn't resist any longer, his yell of pleasure matching hers as, together, they released themselves to the moment.

Chapter Fourteen

For the first time in a long time he woke with a smile, the kind of smile that started deep in his soul and affected far more than his lips. Stretching his arms over his head, Kyle looked around Betsy's sun-dappled bedroom. Somehow, during the night, they'd made it upstairs, their bodies exhausted from a second and third round of lovemaking.

For days he'd been entertaining a host of erotic fantasies starring his next-door neighbor, wild images that had left him torn between want and fear. But no more. The reality that was Betsy Anderson—both in and out of the bedroom—blew every single one of those fantasies out of the water and left him wanting more.

There was something about Betsy that gave him hope. Hope that maybe a second chance was possible. Just the way she worried about him made his heart twist in an unfamiliar way. Lila had only cared about herself—her needs, her desires, her dreams, her image. Betsy, on the other hand, cared about him and Callie. She worried about them and took measures to keep them safe.

He stared at the ceiling as he strained to hear some semblance of sound that would cue him to Betsy's whereabouts, but there was nothing. Nothing except the sound of his own heartbeat as he recalled the way they'd made love again and again throughout the night, his internal wall crumbling with each kiss, each touch they shared.

There were no two ways about it. He'd fallen for Betsy Anderson and he'd fallen hard. And, in all honesty, it was easy to see why.

First, she was breathtakingly beautiful in that girl-next-door kind of way. The kind of woman that made heads turn again and again.

Second, she was sweet—plain and simple. She listened when people spoke, considered feelings when expressed and made a point of correcting mistakes.

And, finally, she was talented, and caring, and fun, and creative and amazing in bed.

Sitting up, Kyle swung his legs to the ground and reached for his jeans, the memory of Betsy's hands removing them making him hard all over again.

He wandered into the hall only to stop outside the bathroom door and listen. But there was nothing—nothing except the faint sound of tapping somewhere in the distance. Confident now of her whereabouts, Kyle wound his way past the family room and kitchen and onto the sunporch, the sight of Betsy's scantily clad form rooting his feet just inside the doorway.

"Good morning, sleepyhead." Looking up from her computer screen, she smiled at him, the sparkle in her eyes confirming what he hoped to be true. "Do you like bacon and eggs?"

He knew he was staring but he couldn't help himself. It didn't matter whether she wore a cute summer top with a tight pair of jeans, or a satiny negligee that barely covered all her parts…Betsy was beautiful.

"I could make French toast if you'd rather." She

pressed something on the keyboard and then rose to her feet, gliding up alongside him as if she was made to be there forever. "Pancakes are always an option, too."

He opened his arms and she stepped inside, her head nestling against his chest as his lips found her hair. For a long moment they simply stood there, their bodies pressed against each other once again.

Finally, he spoke, his voice husky with desire once again. "Are *you* an option?"

She looked up at him, her brows furrowed. "Aren't you starving? Especially after…" Her voice trailed off as she rested her head on his chest once again, a hint of a smile brushing against his skin.

"Of course I'm starving. But you're a million times better than any breakfast item you can name." He planted a kiss on her head then released her just enough to make eye contact, his body reacting immediately.

She gently placed a finger over his mouth. "I'm not going anywhere…I promise. But, if it's okay, I'd like to make you something to eat. You never told me what happened with the bridge."

He considered protesting, pondered the notion of using his mouth to sway her to his line of thinking, but he didn't. She deserved to know what happened especially since she'd been the one to call the department's attention to the warning in the first place. "Okay, but that doesn't mean I've given up on the idea of taking you back to bed with me. You are, after all, entirely irresistible."

Rising up on tiptoe, she whispered her lips across his, the tingling sensation of her skin making him second-guess his decision. But before he could say so, she pulled him in the direction of the kitchen. "Are you a coffee guy?"

"Nah. More of a milk and OJ guy."

"I can accommodate that." She winked at him then pointed at the table for two that was positioned under the room's solitary window. "I'll get everything ready... and you just sit. I spent all of last evening dreaming up worst-case scenarios and I can't wait any longer."

"I worried you that much?"

She turned her back to him but not before he noted the slump to her shoulders as she pulled open the refrigerator. His eyes roamed over her as she bent at the waist to retrieve a carton of orange juice and several eggs from their holder. He swallowed back the desire to ravage her where she stood.

"Please don't worry about me. Really, I'm okay."

"I know. It's just going to take me a little time to accept that."

"I understand." And he did. The heart was a funny thing. It could make you retreat behind a rock-solid wall one minute and then lead you into a place you vowed you'd never go again. "You did the right thing yesterday."

"Oh, thanks. Maybe I'm not just a selfish person who cared only about myself?"

He jumped to his feet. Grabbing hold of her arm, he turned her to him, his gaze seeking hers. "I was a jerk the other night. I know that. And I'm sorry. I think we both have ghosts we're trying to slay and you got caught in the knife's path. I'm sorry."

"I forgave you sometime yesterday afternoon," she whispered.

"How? I didn't see you until last night...."

Shrugging, she stepped back against the counter, her

hands finding his waist and guiding him toward her. "I realized you were acting from a place of hurt. We both are. Once I was able to admit that, I couldn't be angry anymore."

For a long moment he simply studied her, his eyes searching her face for any indication that she was simply too good to be true. But there was nothing. Nothing except her sweet smile and compassion-filled eyes. "I—I love you, Betsy."

The surprise in her face was nothing compared to the surprise he felt as the words slipped effortlessly from his mouth. He hadn't intended to say it, hadn't realized he was even truly there yet. But now that he'd put words to the feeling, he knew it to be true.

He loved her. He truly loved her.

She looked up at him through tear-dappled lashes, her smile wobbly. "I love you, too, Kyle. It's why I've been so scared. Don't you see? My heart is involved now."

Wrapping his arms around her, he pulled her to his chest once again. "But don't *you* see? Knowing that only intensifies my need to think with my head, to make smart decisions based on my training."

It wasn't until her shoulders began to move that he realized she was crying. And, for a moment, he considered trying to thwart the tears. But, in the end, he let them flow, his fingers brushing them from her face from time to time. When she was done, she looked up at him and smiled. "Thank you."

"For what?" he asked, his gaze riveted on her face.

"For understanding."

He swallowed over the lump in his throat. "I think you're the one who's done a better job of understanding. But that's about to change. You have my word."

With one last swipe at her damp cheeks, Betsy

gestured toward the table once again. "I'm never going to get your breakfast made if you keep touching me."

"That's okay," he teased.

"Sit."

He sat.

As she made breakfast, he talked, filling her in on the graffiti and the bottle of spray paint they found less than a hundred yards away. It was the tip they'd been waiting for, especially when Jake Morgan at the hardware store was able to give basic details of the person who'd bought the can not more than twenty-four hours earlier. Slowly but surely, the case was coming together.

"It must have been hard to leave last night," she said as she placed a plate of bacon and eggs in front of him. "I mean, to get the first real lead and have to leave…"

"I didn't *have* to leave," he said as he forked a bite of eggs and stopped it just shy of his mouth. "I wanted to leave. To see you."

Her mouth gaped open, making him laugh. "Don't look so surprised. As I said, you're irresistible."

The tears from earlier resurfaced in her eyes, her mouth trembling. Dropping his fork to his plate, he reached across the table and took hold of her hand. "I knew Tom could handle things. He's the best partner a cop could ask for. If something came up, he'd call me."

She nodded but said nothing, her head tilted downward.

"I wanted to see you…to apologize for my behavior the night before and to thank you for distracting Callie away from the graffiti."

Her head snapped up. "Angela told you that part?"

"Of course she did."

"I—I think I was able to convince Callie the words meant something else."

The worry in her eyes touched him deeply and he squeezed her hand. "Callie is fine. I called my mom right after I talked to Angela. Whatever you said worked because she left the park, talking about some little boy from her class."

"Peter."

"Peter?" he repeated.

"The little boy from her class. They played together on the playground while I called Angela."

He shook his head in awe. "I'm her father and I can't remember the name of more than two kids in her class. You're with her for a few minutes and can remember the name of some kid she plays with."

Slipping her hand out from underneath his, she placed it on top. "You attend to the important stuff, Kyle...her happiness, her safety, her well-being. Remembering a name is the easy part."

"I feel like I've abandoned her lately, shoved her off on my mom time after time." He closed his eyes, savored the sense of calm her touch brought to his soul. "But it's the only way I can see fit to keeping her safe."

"And it's smart." Removing her hand from his, she pushed her own plate off to the side. "I imagine you have the day off, right?"

"Normally I wouldn't, but Tom and I swapped with another team a few days ago. Besides—" he glanced up at the clock and grinned "—if I didn't, I'd have had an irate call from the lieutenant by now."

"Let's do something special with Callie."

He stared at her. "Seriously?"

"Seriously."

"Don't you have to write?"

She picked up her plate as she stood. "I did a little writing while you were sleeping. It'll be enough for today."

"Have I told you I love you in the last minute or so?" he asked.

"In the last minute...no."

"I love you, Betsy Anderson."

HE LEANED AGAINST THE TREE to catch his breath, Callie's giggles interspersed with Betsy's whispered pleas for quiet bringing a smile to his lips. Girls were lousy at playing hide-and-seek.

Big or little, females avoided the really clever places to hide like trash cans, sewers and drainage tunnels, opting instead for the standard choices—trees, furniture, bushes. Betsy and Callie were no exception.

Still, he waited, the easy rapport between his daughter and Betsy something to be savored and enjoyed. For as long as he could remember, his mother had been a firm believer in the one-door-closed/one-door-opened way of thinking. And, for the first time in more years than he could count, he believed it, as well.

Lila wasn't meant to be more than the woman who carried Callie. He could see that now. A mother was someone who listened. Someone who nurtured and encouraged a child in all aspects of life. His ex-wife simply didn't fit the bill.

Sliding his back along the trunk, he dropped to the grass beneath the tree, eavesdropping on the two females in his life rather than trying to catch them.

"Are you almost done with your book?" Callie asked, her sweet voice echoing in his ears.

"Not yet. I have about ten more weeks to get it

done." Betsy's whispered words made him sit up, listen closer

"And then they put it in the bookstore?"

"No, not quite. It actually takes about nine months for that process to happen. But at least my part—for the time being—will be done."

Her part. The writing part. The part that had her renting the Rileys' home.

Scrubbing his hand across his face, he leaned against the tree as reality wiped the stars from his eyes. Three months from now Betsy would be gone—headed back to New York and her big writing career. Cedar Creek wasn't her home. It was a pit stop, a writing refuge on the heels of a tough year.

The realization hit with a one-two punch.

What had he been thinking? Who had he been kidding? Betsy's aspirations were bigger than Cedar Creek.

Swallowing back the bile that rose in his throat, he pushed off the ground, his stellar seeking skills finding his daughter in mere seconds.

Eyes wide with excitement, Callie began jumping in place. "We almost had you, didn't we, Daddy?"

"Almost, pumpkin." Turning from his daughter, he pinned Betsy with a hard stare, his voice taking on a wooden quality. "Almost. But fortunately for both of us I wised up just in time."

Chapter Fifteen

It was no use. She simply wasn't hungry.

"I'm sorry, Angela, I really am, but I just can't eat. It looks good but...I'm just not in the mood."

Angela waved her hand in the air then wrapped it around the wineglass in front of her. "I can't blame you. Kyle is playing head games with you right now and it's completely unacceptable." Leaning forward across the table, the woman looked around the outdoor café for a moment before focusing her attention squarely on Betsy. "I admire Kyle for many things—his loyalty to my husband both in and out of the department, his love for his mother and his unwavering devotion to Callie. But this? It's too much."

She had to agree. This one step forward, two steps back stuff was getting tiresome. Not to mention painful. Especially now, after everything they'd shared. "I thought we'd finally reached some, I don't know, understanding, maybe? We're both colored by our past and we're aware of that. But I thought after the other night, after we made love, that things would be—"

Horrified she'd spoken aloud, Betsy clamped her mouth shut, her hand instinctively reaching for the untouched glass of wine beside her untouched plate of food. The last thing she wanted was to be peppered with questions that would force her to relive the most magical night of her life. Not now, when the magic seemed more like a fool's decision.

But it was too late. Angela's eyes widened as her glass smacked down on the table. "You were together? The other night? I knew it! I knew it was going to happen... you two are perfect for each other."

"No. We're not." Propping her elbow beside her plate, she rested her chin on the backside of her hand. "I wish we were, I really do. But we're not. A relationship that's truly meant to be shouldn't be this hard."

Angela's brows furrowed. "How do you mean?"

She tried her best to explain, to put words to the revelation-of-sorts she'd reached over the past twelve months. "Well, if two people are truly right for each other it shouldn't be so hard. Compromise is good— don't get me wrong. But if the whole thing is compromise, someone is going through the motions all the time. A true relationship, one that's meant to be, shouldn't be like that."

"You seemed to work together pretty effortlessly when we played volleyball."

"Well, we certainly seem to have similar interests in terms of what we like to do—visits to the park, barbecuing with friends..."

"Romantic backyard picnics?"

Her face warmed at the memory. "You know about that?"

"I think the entire Cedar Creek police force and their spouses know about that picnic." Angela made a face. "And I know I wasn't the only spouse who was asked why we don't do stuff like that."

She laughed. "Sorry. But I owed him an apology

and it didn't appear as if he was going to give me an opportunity to give the standard verbal variety. I needed to take drastic measures."

Breaking off a bite-size piece of bread from her plate, Angela nodded, an unreadable expression crossing her face. "So spending time together—in terms of what you like to do—is fairly effortless already?"

"Absolutely. With Mark, it was a constant study in compromise from the very beginning. Though, in all fairness, the compromise only came after the arguments."

"He wanted to hang out in bars all the time?" Angela asked, a knowing smile lifting her lips.

"Uh-huh."

"And you went along with it for a while...tried to embrace that life because you thought you should?"

"Uh-huh."

"And when you finally said something, he made a token effort only to slip back to his usual behavior?"

She felt her mouth gape open. "How'd you know that?"

Angela shrugged. "It's the way it was with just about every guy I dated before Tom." With a quick hand the copper-haired spitfire pushed the bread into her mouth. When she'd finished chewing, she continued on. "But, if I'm hearing you correctly, you're not picking that up with Kyle. Right?"

"Not at all."

"O-kay...so where's the part that's not effortless?"

Lifting her chin off her hand, she leaned back against the wire-mesh patio chair. "Everything else. My fear over his job, his concern that I'm going to up and walk out on him at the drop of a hat one day. And yesterday—" she exhaled a sigh of frustration "—I have no idea what went wrong there. One minute we're playing hide-and-seek in the park and Callie and I are waiting for him to find us. When he finally shows up, he's carrying an attitude that came out of nowhere. It's too much."

"Ahh." Angela pushed her plate to the side and leaned forward. "You have no idea where the attitude came from?"

"No. He just showed up with a poorly veiled innuendo regarding my ability to stick around."

"Your ability to stick around?"

As silly as it sounded out in the open, it was all she'd been able to come up with to explain the irrefutable shift in Kyle's mood halfway through their outing with Callie. "One minute things are great and the next, he's practically volunteering to help me pack my bags."

For a moment Angela said nothing. She simply sat there, looking down at her hands. Finally, though, she spoke, her voice uncharacteristically subdued. "If you knew a breakup was coming, don't you think you'd find it less painful if you were part of the process rather than watching, blindsided, from the side of the road?"

"Of course. It's what made me want to give up on any notion of a relationship with Kyle. If *I* cut it off, then it would be my own doing. If I lost him because of some horrible tragedy, well, it would just be harder. Because I'd be unprepared."

"And you don't think he feels the same way?"

The meaning behind Angela's cryptic statement hit her full force. She and Callie had been talking about the book. "Oh, I get it now."

And she did. He knew her stay in Cedar Creek was tied to her work. When the writing was done, there'd be nothing to keep her here.

"What matters, though, is that none of this is insurmountable." Angela, too, leaned back in her seat, her fingers finding the stem of her wineglass and giving it a swirl. "It's really just a matter of jumping a few hurdles. The kind of hurdles you'll jump for the rest of your life for one reason or another. But as long as you know they're there, and you do your best to jump them together, they won't be such a big deal."

She nodded, her mind registering Angela's words and commanding them to memory. "How did you get to be so smart with all of this?"

Ang shrugged. "There are times when Tom carries me, and there are times when I carry him, but we listen to one another *always*. And we respect each other's feelings above all else. It's the only way."

She met her friend's gaze head-on. "A week ago, when I rented my place, I knew it was temporary."

"And now?"

"I don't know." And she didn't. "New York is my home. Or, at least it was."

The left corner of Angela's mouth lifted, followed by the right. "Was?"

"Was…is…I'm not sure. The way I feel for Kyle is enough to make me want to stay here forever. But— " she stared out into the distance as reality reared its head "—this constant push-pull? This feeling as if I'm being blamed for something I didn't do? I can't live like that… and I won't."

"SO WE'VE GOT NOTHING?" Kyle asked as his fist hit the locker. "C'mon, Jake gave a description of the guy, didn't he?"

Tom dropped onto the bench at the end of the locker

room. "He did. But, as of now, it hasn't turned anything up yet. The key word is *yet.*"

"Are we waiting until one of these losers breaks into my mother's home and takes off with my kid?"

"What the hell is with you, dude? There's not a guy in this department who doesn't have his ear to the ground for anything that might shed light on who these guys are. Guys are working extra hours, driving past your house at all hours of the day and night, driving their personal vehicles into the outskirts of town late at night. Why? Because we want this stopped as much as you do. For you and your kid."

There was no denying the anger in Tom's voice. It was an emotion his partner rarely exuded outside of football season. But it was there now, and it was more than a little justified.

Resting his forehead against the cool metal of his locker, he closed his eyes, willed the tension in his body to ease. "Look, I'm sorry. I was out of line just now."

"You're damn straight you were." Tom pitched himself forward as he rested his elbows on his thighs. "It's only a matter to of time, dude. We'll get 'em."

"I'm just worried. My daughter saw that graffiti."

"But Betsy smoothed it over. It's okay."

Betsy.

Just the sound of her name made his heart race and his stomach churn. How could one person make you feel as high as a kite one moment and like dirt the next? "It's not her job to smooth things over. It's mine."

"I get that. But be glad she was there."

"At that moment, yes. But she won't be for much longer."

Tom stared at him. "What are you babbling about?"

Cocking his head against the locker, he stared up at the ceiling, the white stucco finish in desperate need of a paint job. "Betsy, who else?"

"I got that. What's this about her not being around for much longer?"

His eyes fixed on a round water stain that appeared relatively new. "This isn't her home, Tom. New York is. She's only here so she can write her book."

"And?"

"When her book is finished, she goes back." Without waiting for a response, he continued on, his mouth finally putting words to the nagging thoughts that had kept him awake half the night. "I've already accepted the fact that I'm an idiot—that I seem to be a glutton for punishment."

"Oh?"

He nodded. "My choice in women. At first, when I heard what Betsy did for a living, I likened her to Lila and that was unfair. I realize that now. Betsy is more grounded, more real. But that doesn't mean I'm blind. She's a writer—a fairly popular one at that. And, unless I'm mistaken, New York is where it's at for publishing, isn't it? She's not gonna give that up for me. Who would? Does it hurt? Hell, yeah. But I'm a big boy. Callie is just a little girl."

"What does this have to do with Callie?"

"Sometimes I'm so wrapped up in my own world I forget that I'm not the only one who got hurt by Lila walking the way she did. That little girl lost her mother. Her *mother,* Tom." He pulled his gaze from the ceiling and fixed it on his partner. "And what did I do? I served my daughter's heart on a silver platter to a woman who doesn't consider Cedar Creek her home any more than Lila did. I'm not sure I can forgive myself for that one."

"You lost me, dude."

He tried again. "I should have known better as far as my heart was concerned. Hell, I *do* know better. But I ignored it and plowed ahead anyway, dragging Callie into my mistake by my own two hands."

Tom's left eyebrow rose, and then his right. "Wait, let me get this straight. You've decided Betsy is leaving when her book is done. And because she's spent some time with Callie over the past week or so, you've decided your child will be forever damaged when she leaves?"

Listening to his thought process aloud made him squirm. "I think you're oversimplifying things a bit, but, yeah."

"I'm not oversimplifying. I'm just giving the Cliffs Notes version. I'm a master at encapsulating ten minutes into thirty seconds." Tom rose to pace around the locker room. "Has Betsy said she's leaving the second the book is done?"

He followed his friend around the room, watching with amusement as Tom opened lockers in search of superfluous snacks. "Not recently, but—"

"Then why are you so sure she's leaving?" In the third locker he came to, Tom hit the jackpot with an open bag of individually wrapped chocolate squares. Popping one into his mouth, he peered over his shoulder at Kyle. "You don't think Hanson will mind, do you?"

"I doubt he'll notice one or two…or three missing candies." Kyle shook his head. "I'm sure she's leaving because she *lives* in New York, Tom. She's just here temporarily."

Tom closed Hanson's locker then switched to the other side of the room, his fingers deftly opening and closing each door. "I'm pretty sure she can write from anywhere. There are authors all over this country who live in places other than New York. That's one of the many beauties of computers, e-mail and an occasional airplane ticket."

Was Tom right? Could Betsy really work from anywhere?

"Seriously, stop borrowing trouble and just see how things play out." Tom gave up his search and headed toward the door. "You've got feelings for her—that's obvious. So why not see where they go?"

Oh, he knew where they went. And how they tasted. And how they felt. And how they sounded. And how they moved. It was all he'd thought about since they were together.

Well, that, and the nagging voice in his head warning him to get out before it was too late.

To Tom, he simply shrugged. "That's all well and good except for one thing."

"What's that?"

"Callie."

His hand on the door, Tom turned. "Callie was six months old when Lila left. She remembers nothing. And unless I'm missing something, she's one well-adjusted kid despite that." Releasing his grip on the door, Tom crossed his arms in front of his chest. "Second, there's not a single one of us who can't benefit from feeling special even if it's only for a little while. Betsy does that for Callie."

"Yeah, but—"

"But nothing. You don't know Betsy is leaving. If she does, you deal with it then. Quit borrowing trouble before you have to."

Chapter Sixteen

There were times she questioned her own judgment. But, in those instances, it usually involved a character or a plot point—mundane stuff that could be deleted and changed without anyone being the wiser.

Today, though, there would be no opportunity to delete, no chance to sweep a mistake under the proverbial carpet. Because this time her error in judgment extended to the real world.

Betsy set the tray of piping hot cookies onto a wire rack and then leaned against the counter, her eyes seeking the clock on the microwave again and again. Tom and Angela, along with Kyle and Callie, were due at her home in less than five minutes and every warning bell in her head was sounding.

What on earth was she trying to prove? Kyle had relationship issues, that was obvious. But he reached for old answers when question marks reared between them. And it wasn't fair.

She wasn't Lila.

And he's not Mark….

The thought brought her up short. She'd done the same thing to him. She'd used the past to dictate her present.

But was it a habit they could break?

A knock at the front door brought an end to her misgivings. With a quick wipe of her hand on a nearby dish towel, Betsy peeked around the corner of the kitchen and waved her friends inside. "Hi, Angela. Hi, Tom. C'mon in."

Angela stepped in first, her green catlike eyes set off perfectly by the green T-shirt and white capris she sported. Behind her came Tom, decked out in a pair of long black nylon shorts and a cream-colored shirt boasting a favorite beer label.

"Mmm, do I smell chocolate chip cookies?"

She couldn't help but laugh at the way Tom's nose rose into the air to chase the homemade scent. "Yes."

"Kudos to my wife, here, for finding such a good friend." Stopping just inside the kitchen doorway, he pointed at the tray. "Did you know that royalty often have taste testers?"

"Oh, here we go." Angela folded her arms across her chest and rolled her eyes.

Ignoring his wife, Tom continued. "The taste tester is there to make sure that all food is fit for consumption before it touches the lips of royalty. That way, if someone tries to poison the king via his food, the taste tester will die first, alerting the king to danger and thus, saving his life."

The corners of her mouth twitched as she shot a knowing look in Angela's direction before addressing Tom. "So...why, exactly, are you telling me this?"

His face a mask of seriousness, Tom looked at the cookies and then back at Betsy. "It would be a shame to see something happen to you. Your fans would be crushed. Don't you think you owe it to them to take certain precautions?"

Uncrossing her arms, Angela marched across the kitchen and pulled a cookie from the tray. "He wants a cookie. And unless you want puppy dog eyes following you for the rest of the day you need to let him have one. Now."

At Betsy's amused nod, Tom reached for the cookie and shoved it into his mouth, his eyes closing in satisfaction. "This is why I love my wife."

"Hey! I'm the one who made those cookies, mister," Betsy protested, her words morphing into laughter. Maybe it really was going to be okay. Even if Kyle showed up with his stone-faced persona, she'd still have fun thanks to Angela and Tom.

A second knock at the door made them all turn, the quick look of amusement between Angela and Tom not lost on her.

"In gratitude for that cookie, I'll get the door," Tom said as he patted Betsy on the back. "Give me another and you won't even know he's here."

"You're on," she quipped as she scooped a second cookie from the tray and handed it to Angela's husband.

"Man, you're easy."

She pulled her gaze from Tom's back as it receded down the hallway and fixed it on Angela. "I shouldn't have invited him."

"Yes, you should have." Grabbing hold of Betsy's arm, Angela pulled her onto the sunporch. "These are just hurdles, Betsy. Hurdles can be jumped."

"Can they? When they keep popping up again and again?"

"You know you want to," Angela said before turning to greet Callie as the little girl ran down the hall, her father trailing behind Tom. "Callie, I love those braids! Think you can do that to my hair one day?"

Callie laughed, a contagious sound that made them all smile. Even Kyle. "Your hair is too short for braids, Mrs. Murphy. But Ashley in my class wears lots of little ponytails in her hair. Maybe that would work on your hair, too."

Stepping onto the sunporch, Tom shooed Callie forward toward the back door and the lawn games he'd dropped off earlier in the day. "I think we should leave that style for Ashley. Let it be her special thing. What do you say?"

If Callie answered, they didn't hear, her long braids smacking against her shoulders as she followed Tom into the backyard.

"Hey, Ang." Kyle touched the woman's shoulder with his hand, planting a gentle kiss on her cheek at the same time. When he straightened up, he looked at Betsy, his eyes conveying things she was afraid to decipher. "Hi, Betsy. Thanks for inviting us. My mom said Callie's been talking about it all morning." Glancing down at the container in his hand, he extended it in her direction. "I made up a batch of cheddar and bacon potatoes. I hope you like them."

"You didn't have to do that. I know you're busy at the station."

"And you're busy writing." He took a step forward as he spoke, the gap between them growing smaller by the moment. "It's no different."

It never ceased to amaze her how her body sprang to attention the moment Kyle was near. It was as if her very being was equipped with an invisible homing mechanism where he was concerned.

"You know, I think I'm going to head outside. See if

maybe Tom and Callie need a little help with whatever they've gotten themselves into."

Angela's words broke through her reverie, returning her to the reality that was her relationship with Kyle. "Why don't you both go outside? I'll be out in a minute after I put these potatoes in the oven to warm."

The disappointment in Kyle's face was mirrored in Angela's but neither made an issue of her request. Instead, they dutifully did as they were asked, leaving her alone inside the kitchen.

She appreciated Angela's efforts to give them privacy, she really did. But she simply wasn't ready. The hurt was still too raw.

Fortunately it didn't last for long. In addition to his many endearing traits, Tom Murphy was a master at making people feel at ease. His sunny disposition, coupled with his goofy sense of humor, had them laughing away the hours as they alternated between dinner, lawn darts, dessert, volleyball and, finally, good old conversation set against the backdrop of a portable fireplace and a platter of s'more fixings.

"So...do you think you'll make your deadline?"

Startled, she looked up from the s'more Callie was making, and met Angela's eyes. Why on earth would she bring that up now? Especially when things with Kyle were going so well?

"Uh...I hope so. I kind of need to."

"What happens after it's written?" Kyle asked from his spot on the other side of the picnic table. "I mean, do you start on the next one?"

Buoyed by his sudden interest, she took the opportunity to bring clarity to an unfamiliar picture. "Ideally? Yes, I'd start on the next one. But, realistically? That doesn't always happen. For the first few weeks after I finish, I'm running around getting caught up on all the things that got shoved aside while my face was pressed to the keyboard—appointments, reestablishing contact with friends, cleaning, you name it."

"Angela forgets to clean sometimes, too, but I'm not sure what her excuse is," Tom quipped only to release a groan as his wife's elbow met the side of his stomach.

Shaking his head, Kyle gestured to Betsy. "Go on."

"I also use that time to rid my mind of the fictional world I just completed so it can be ready for the next one. For me that means reading for the first time in months, or seeing movies. Or going for long walks in the park, that sort of thing."

"There's some great walking trails down by Paxton Bridge," Angela offered, her meaning not lost on Betsy even without the accompanying wink.

"Then what?"

She looked back at Kyle. "Then I start writing again."

"But what about the book you've just finished? Aren't there commitments tied to that one even after you turn it in?"

"Sure. There are a few rounds of edits prior to production, and book signings, interviews and speaking engagements after. But the after-stuff only lasts a few weeks."

"Sounds like a pretty good job for someone with a family, doesn't it, Kyle?"

Nibbling back the laugh that threatened to escape, Betsy bowed her head only to peek up at Kyle through long lashes as he stared at his partner. "I guess…"

Taking the ball from her husband, Angela planted a quick kiss on Callie's head. "Seriously, so other than two, maybe three weeks of traveling when the book releases, you're home? Writing? Or getting caught up on other things?"

She felt Kyle's eyes on her as she pondered her answer. In the end, she simply reiterated the truth as Angela had summed it up. "Exactly. And when I haven't been facing writer's block for a year, I don't play my deadlines quite so close. Which means I write for a few hours each day and never really face a huge crunch time like I am now."

"Pretty cool, huh, partner?" Tom ducked as Kyle chucked a marshmallow at his head. "What? What? I just said it was cool. What's wrong with that?"

Rising from her spot at the table, Angela began gathering plates and cups. "As wonderful as this has been, I'm going to have to be a party pooper and call it a night. I've been dragging lately and if I don't leave now I'm going to fall asleep on the graham crackers."

Betsy jumped up, her hand stilling Angela's mid-clean. "I can get this. Really. All that's left is the s'more stuff."

"Yeah, you guys go on ahead. I'll help Betsy get the rest of this inside."

"Cool." Tom pointed at Callie. "Can I help with her, at least?"

They all laughed as they looked at Kyle's daughter, the little girl's head pillowed in her hand as she slept soundly beside her half-eaten s'more.

"Sure." Kyle stood by as Tom lifted Callie into his arms then hurried ahead to hold Betsy's back door open. "Why don't you set her down on the couch in the family room for now."

"It's okay if you want to take her all the way home now," Betsy protested as she followed behind them.

"Really, I can handle the rest of the cleanup myself. There's not much left."

"No. I'm not leaving you out here alone at night."

Kyle's tone, kind yet firm, wiped any further objection from her lips. "Okay."

When Angela and Tom had left, and the door was safely closed, Kyle cornered her in the kitchen. "I'm sorry about the other day at the park. I guess I let fear win again. My feelings for you are stronger than anything I've ever felt and—"

"Ever?" she whispered with surprise.

"Ever." He reached out, placed his hands on her hips and pulled her toward him. "And the realization that you'll be gone in less than three months took me by surprise."

She opened her mouth to speak only to be stopped by his finger. "I love you, Betsy, and I'm willing to see where that can take us. I really am. I just don't want Callie getting hurt."

"I wouldn't hurt Callie!"

"I believe that's the case...at least not intentionally. But it could happen."

Rising up on tiptoes, Betsy nuzzled her nose against Kyle's chin, the warmth of his skin bringing a moan of pleasure to her lips. "It won't. We just need to jump together. As a team. It's the only way."

"No surprises?" he asked, his gaze finding hers and holding it.

"No surprises."

Chapter Seventeen

"Betsy? It's Hannah."

Grateful for the reprieve, Betsy positioned the cursor and pressed Save. "Hi, Hannah. How are you?"

For as long as she could recall, she and Hannah had been more like friends than business partners, their agent/writer relationship a rarity from everything she'd heard. Perhaps it was the fact that they were similar in age and thus understood a little bit about the pressures that entailed. Perhaps it was their common love for New York and the vast cultural life that spoke to both of them. Perhaps it was their shared interest in books and authors that gave them fodder for hour-long phone conversations.

Or perhaps it was a combination of all three. But whatever it was, or wasn't, she was simply grateful for the woman on the other end of the line.

"I'm not sure."

With radar on high alert, she stood and walked to the window, her gaze instinctively finding the gap in the hedge that forged a makeshift path straight to Kyle's house. "You're not sure? What does that mean?"

Her agent sighed in her ear. "Well, it depends on how you react."

Uh-oh.

"Tell me they're not moving up my deadline? C'mon, Hannah…they gave me less than three months!"

"They gave you *twelve* months, Betsy."

She considered arguing but realized it was futile. Hannah was right. They'd given her twelve months. It was she who had squandered it away. "For the hundredth time, I'm sorry. I really am. But if it's any consolation, the story is flowing really well right now. And as long as they don't move it up on me, I have no doubt I can make the first of August."

"Neither do I. And neither does Marsha."

She felt her shoulders relax. "So then if it's not a change to my deadline, what's up?"

"Marsha wants you in her office at nine o'clock tomorrow morning."

"Nine o'clock? Hannah, I can't!" She spun around and headed toward the kitchen. "How can they expect me to make deadline if I'm flying halfway across the country for—for…for what, exactly?"

"A prep session."

Hannah's words sent her radar pinging. "A prep session for what?"

"For your interview."

Stopping in the middle of the kitchen, Betsy looked around, a sudden craving for chocolate leaving her wide-eyed and desperate.

Now where did those chocolate bars from last night end up?

"Isn't it a bit premature for interviews when I haven't even finished the book?" She wandered over to the cabinet beside the refrigerator and flung it open. Nothing.

"Well, this particular story wouldn't be about the book, exactly."

She tried the cabinet to the left. Nothing again. "What, exactly, would it be about then?"

Hannah's responding sigh made her fling open the cabinet beside the stove, her gaze falling on the stack of three chocolate bars.

Oh, thank heavens...

"Are you sitting down?"

She shook her head then repeated the sentiment into the phone as she unwrapped the first bar.

"Are you eating chocolate?"

Breaking a small rectangle from the first bar, Betsy popped it into her mouth. "You know what? It's almost scary how well you know me. But wait...you know I need chocolate when I'm stressed."

Silence filled her ear.

"What's going on? What is this interview about?" she asked, her voice rising despite the chocolate she continued to stuff in her mouth.

"The house feels that your readers have gone too long without a book from you. That there's a chance their interest might wane."

"I'm typing as fast as I can. I really am."

"I know that. And so does Marsha. But it will still be almost a year until it comes out."

She unwrapped the second bar. "Okay..."

"Which means a gap of two years since the last book."

"So?" she prompted as she moved her free hand in a circular motion her agent couldn't see.

"The house feels that's unacceptable."

"But you just said Marsha was okay with the deadline." She could feel her hands beginning to tremble. Pulling the fridge open, she grabbed a carton of milk and set it on the counter. "How can it suddenly be un-acceptable?"

Hannah rushed to explain. "It's not the agreed-upon deadline that's unacceptable. It's the gap between books."

She considered bypassing a glass in favor of whacking her head against the cabinet, but she opted for the glass instead. "You've lost me."

"The house wants you in front of your readers *now*. To remind them you're still out there. To build their anticipation."

Uh-oh.

"You mean, they want to exploit what happened with Mark?"

"*Exploit* is a bit harsh, don't you think?"

"No. I don't. That's the focus they want this interview to take, isn't it?" She poured herself half a glass of milk, downing it in short fashion.

"That's the whole point behind the prep session with Marsha beforehand. To find out what questions you're comfortable with and what questions you're not."

Setting her glass back on the counter, she leaned against the refrigerator and closed her eyes, memories she'd finally tucked away resurfacing with a vengeance. "What happens if I'm not comfortable with the whole idea of this interview?"

Again, there was silence.

"Hannah? Are you still there?"

"Yeah, I'm still here."

"Well, what if I don't want to do the interview?"

"I'm not sure either of us wants to know that answer, Betsy."

And she was probably right. As much as she hated the notion of opening her pain to strangers, it was the consequence for neglecting her career in the way she had. The publishing house was about the bottom line. If she wanted to continue writing—for them or anyone else—she had to care about it, as well. Even when the bottom line threatened to reopen wounds that had finally begun to heal.

"Okay. I'll do it. But I will veto any question I feel is inappropriate or unnecessary. And I expect that my veto will be honored."

"It will be," Hannah assured. "If you want me in that prep meeting with you, I'll be there."

"Nine o'clock, you said?" She glanced at the clock, mentally calculating how quickly she'd need to move in order to be sitting in her editor's office the next morning.

"I have you on a five-fifteen flight out of O'Hare," Hannah volunteered.

"Oh, you do, do you?"

"And I have a car picking you up at your house at one-thirty."

"One-thirty? I can't make that!"

"Of course you can. What's it there? Ten?"

"Ten-fifteen."

"You can type on the plane."

Pushing off the counter, she wandered over to the still-open candy cabinet and shut the door. "Okay."

"Did you say okay?"

"Yes."

"Thank you, Betsy."

"It's no big deal. It's just a day, right?"

Silence.

"Hannah?"

"Two, actually."

She opened the cabinet once again. "Why two? Isn't this interview right after the prep session?"

"Um...the first one is."

"The first one? You mean, there's more?"

"There are three, actually. A print one, a radio one and a TV one."

Grabbing the third candy bar, Betsy slammed the cabinet and headed toward the desk in her bedroom where she kept her best stationery. "Okay, fine. But just two days. That's it."

CAREFUL NOT TO STEP ON the freshly planted flowerbed that bordered the side of Betsy's house, Kyle made his way from the front porch to the back. Although they hadn't made any specific plans for the evening, he'd hoped they could hang out for a while and talk. Truth was, the more he got to know Betsy Anderson the more he craved every single solitary second he could have with her.

All day long he'd thought of little else besides his neighbor. The way her hair swished against her back as she walked, the way the corners of her eyes crinkled when she smiled, the way her cheeks flushed when she caught him watching her.

And it felt good. Damn good.

When he reached the back door he cupped his hands to his eyes and peered inside, the darkness in the front end of the house duplicated in the back. Where was she? And why was her car still parked in the driveway?

A hint of unease reared its head as he walked around the far side of the house only to find more of the same. Darkness.

His cell phone vibrated against his skin and he pulled

it from his pants' pocket. With a quick check of the screen, he flipped it open. "What's up, Tom?"

"Nothin' much. Just bored, I guess."

"Oh."

Holding the phone to his ear, he started back toward Betsy's rear door. It, like the front door, was locked, no lights visible anywhere. If something had happened would she have—

"What are you doing?"

Tom. Right. He'd almost forgotten he was holding the phone.

"Right now I'm outside Betsy's back door and I've got a bad feeling."

"What's wrong?" Instantly, the boredom that had laced his partner's voice just seconds earlier was gone. In its place the kind of quick focus he valued in the man both personally and professionally. "Someone break in?"

"No, I don't think so. The windows and doors are all locked. The lights are off."

"Oh. So then what's the problem?"

His attention moved to the vehicle parked in the driveway. "Her car's still here." Raking his free hand through his hair, he willed his head to remain cool. "I don't know. Maybe she went for a run or something... though I don't think she runs."

"No, dude. She's in New York."

"Come again?" he asked.

"She's in New York. She left a few hours ago."

"New York?" he repeated. "Why?"

"Don't know. I just know what Ang told me. Betsy called and asked her to water her plants for the next two days. Something about some interviews or something."

He felt his jaw tighten as the meaning of Tom's words hit home. Betsy had taken off without so much as a call to tell him where she was going and why. Yet she'd found the time to call Angela and make sure her plants were looked after?

"Hey. You still there?"

What an idiot he was for believing all that garbage about being home all the time. What? She'd been in Cedar Creek less than two weeks and she was already jetting off to New York?

"Kyle! You there?"

"Yeah, I'm here." He could hear the anger in his voice but could do nothing to stop it. "Tell me something, Tom…"

"Shoot."

"What does being part of a team mean to you?"

"Seriously?"

"Yeah."

"Sticking together. Having each other's back. Working together. Communicating. Why?"

He closed his eyes. "No reason. I already knew the answer. I just wanted to make sure I wasn't the only one."

"Oh, okay, good. You had me confused for a second there. I think you'd be hard-pressed to find someone who doesn't know what it means."

With one last look over his shoulder, Kyle made his way between the hedge that separated his yard from Betsy's, anger morphing into sadness with each passing step. "Actually, it's not as hard as you might think."

Chapter Eighteen

The first time or two she heard his taped recording, she thought nothing of it. Lots of people stopped by the market and ran errands after work. Add in the fact he had a daughter to care for and his inability to answer the phone made perfect sense.

By the third and fourth time, however, she was starting to wonder.

Glancing at the clock on the nightstand, Betsy flipped open her cell phone once again, Kyle's position on her contact list all but memorized. When she reached his name she pressed Send, the all too familiar succession of rings starting once again.

And once again, as it had all evening, Kyle's phone went to voice mail. There was no ignoring the truth any longer. If his phone were off, it wouldn't take five rings to reach his recording. Which meant he was screening calls and deliberately avoiding hers.

She closed her hand over the phone and snapped it shut, her body sinking back against the splay of pillows that stretched across the hotel bed. It had been a trying day, the kind of day that made a person want to pull the covers over their head until it was all over. But Kyle *was* her covers. He was all she'd thought about during the prep session with Marsha that morning and the television interview that afternoon. In fact, it was the sensation of his arms around her that had gotten her through some of the roughest questions.

Yet now that she finally had an opportunity to call him, to hear his voice, he wanted nothing to do with her or her phone call. But why? Was he angry that she left a note rather than calling?

No. He couldn't be. She'd explained that in the note. He'd been working a double shift when she left, his intended task to track down more information on the suspected gang-member-turned-graffiti-artist. The last thing she'd wanted to do was disrupt his concentration. It made perfect sense.

So then why was he avoiding her? Why was he sending her calls to voice mail and not returning any of them? Had something happened? Had there been a break in the case that prevented him from getting to the phone?

No. Angela would have called. She promised.

Closing her eyes against the tears that threatened to fall, Betsy curled into the fetal position, her mind and body completely spent.

HE WAS HALFWAY UP THE DRIVEWAY before he heard it, a persistent tapping that called his attention to the one place he would have preferred to ignore. Turning his head from the sun, he looked across the yard to Betsy's kitchen, Angela Murphy's hand waving wildly in his direction.

Cranking the window open, the woman flashed her megawatt smile in his direction. "Hey there, Kyle. How are you?"

"Okay. And you?"

"Good…busy." Frowning suddenly, his partner's wife lifted a watering can into the air with one hand and gestured him over with the other. "C'mon over, I don't feel like having the whole neighborhood eavesdropping on our every word."

"Planning on talking dirty to me, Ang?" he asked, a smile tugging at his face in spite of his foul mood.

She stuck her tongue at him. "That's Betsy's job, not mine."

At the mere mention of his neighbor's name he stiffened. A full twenty-four hours after taking off for New York without so much as a word, the calls had started. At first, her messages had been cheerful enough, her sweet voice testing his willpower like never before. On the fifth try, she'd hung up without leaving a message.

And she hadn't tried again.

Which suited him just fine. He had no desire to waste another thought on someone as thoughtless and self-centered as Betsy Anderson. He'd had enough. More than enough, quite frankly.

"Are you coming?" Angela called as she continued to alternate her attention between watering plants and sizing him up. "I can't keep standing at this same window. If I do, I'd be setting myself up on murder charges."

"Murder charges?"

"Yeah. Negligent drowning of innocent plants."

"I'm thinking that wouldn't be much more than a misdemeanor." He took a step closer to the window. "So, when's our resident celebrity coming back?"

"It was supposed to be this evening but her editor shoved another interview at her for tomorrow morning." Angela waved to him once again, this time gesturing him around the back of the house. "Meet me in the back."

His protest went unnoticed as Angela left the window. Sighing, he did as he was told, his feet leading him around a yard he had become all too familiar with the past two weeks. When he reached the back, she was waiting, her free hand holding the door open for him.

"I felt bad that I missed her call this morning, she sounded awful on my machine. But I was at the gym."

"Whatever." He stepped onto the sunporch, his eyes riveted on the empty computer table in the middle of the room. "It's not my problem."

Angela stopped beside the plant cart in the corner of the room and turned around, her eyes pinning his with surprise. "What's not your problem?"

"Betsy. Her mood. Her trip. Her anything," he said, the bitterness in his voice evident to anyone within a ten-mile radius.

"Excuse me?" Angela's eyes narrowed as her hand tightened around the handle of the watering can. "What's this about?"

"What?"

"This…this attitude."

He leaned against the wall only to push himself off it and pace around the room. "Attitude? Attitude? I don't have an attitude. I have anger and lots of it. And rightfully so, if you ask me."

"I see that."

"I had Betsy figured out the moment Tom told me who she was…the *moment* he told me."

Smacking the watering can onto an open shelf, Angela folded her arms across her chest and stared at him. "And what, exactly, did you have figured out, Kyle?"

"That she was self-centered, concerned only with herself and her career. Like my lovely ex-wife."

"Lila? You think Betsy is like Lila?"

"A carbon copy," he spat through clenched teeth. "Three nights ago she sat at that picnic table right out there and painted this elaborate picture of life as a published author. Do you remember that?"

"I do. Do you?"

"You bet I do. And I remember her sitting there, lamenting the fact she only travels for two, maybe three weeks after her book comes out. So much for that, huh?"

Angela's mouth gaped open as anger filled her eyes. "Wait. Let me guess. This last-minute trip to New York makes her a liar?"

"Among other things."

"Such as?"

He continued to pace around the room, the windows and walls fading into the background as he focused on his anger and the reason for it. "After you and Tom left the other night we talked. I allowed myself to get taken in—to believe her when she said she wanted us to be a team. To get over the hurdles of our past together."

The hint of a smile passed across Angela's face. "Hurdles, huh?"

"Yeah."

Waving a dismissive hand in the air, the smile disappeared. "And what makes you think that's changed?"

"I think the fact that she took off for New York without so much as a phone call says enough, don't you?"

"What are you talking about?"

He started pacing again. "She took off. For three days. And I found out from Tom! I think that speaks volumes about where I fall in her life, don't you?"

"Maybe…if it were true." Angela stalked across the room in his direction, her charge barely slowing as she grabbed him by the wrist and pulled him through the back door.

"What the hell, Angela?"

"When's the last time you checked your mailbox?" she asked as her pull became a push the moment they reached the break in the hedge.

"About ten minutes ago."

"And you didn't see it?"

"See what?"

"Betsy's note. She told me she was leaving it in the box beside your door."

He stopped halfway to his back door. "She left a note? In my mailbox?"

"That's what she said." Angela breezed past him en route to his back stoop, her fingers snapping in his direction for the key. "Did you even go through your mail, Kyle?"

Had he? He couldn't remember.

Following his partner's wife into his home, his gaze fell on the pile of mail he'd dropped on the kitchen table—a pile that had increased day by day. When Angela spied it, she rummaged through the ads and envelopes until her hand emerged with a soft-pink envelope that bore his name in flowery handwriting.

"Read it," she commanded.

With a careful finger, he ripped open the top of the envelope and extracted the matching pink note.

Dearest Kyle,

    I received an unexpected call from my agent this morning. It seems as if my publishing house is afraid I've ruined my career by taking so long to finish my next book. In their desire to see that doesn't happen, I've been scheduled for several interviews designed to reconnect me with my readers. These interviews will be quite personal in nature and, I imagine, painful. But I will get through them as quickly as I can knowing I have you to return to when it's all done.

I thought about calling when I got word of this trip but felt a note would be better in light of your overtime shift and your work on the case. I will call you tomorrow evening as soon as my first interview is over.

I miss you and Callie already.

With love,

Betsy

When he reached the bottom of the note, he read it again, a lump forming in his throat as he realized the enormity of his mistake.

"She left without telling you, huh?" Angela retraced her steps to the back door and then stopped. Turning around she pointed a finger at him. "Betsy is special. You better get that through your head before it's too late."

Chapter Nineteen

It never ceased to amaze her how quickly life could change. One minute it could be alive with hope, the next fraught with the kind of reality that squashed hope in its tracks. But she'd learned a lot over the past twelve months.

She'd learned that time stood still for no one—a fact that presented two options. Roll over and let it pass you by or jump in and do the best you can.

For months she'd done the former—losing herself and her dreams in the process. And it had cost her dearly, robbing her of the one thing everyone needed.

Hope.

Without hope, there was nothing. And that was something she didn't intend to experience ever again.

Allowing herself just one last look at the break in the hedge that separated her home from Kyle's, she inhaled slowly, deeply. Writing was her dream. It always had been. And while she truly believed she could continue to live that dream *and* be in a loving and committed relationship, Kyle, apparently, did not.

His loss.

She had a book to write. And a home to return to.

Neither of which could happen soon enough as far as she was concerned.

Turning her back to the window once and for all, Betsy made her way over to the computer table and the work in progress that awaited her on the screen. Slowly but surely, her fingers took over, the story she'd crafted in her head finding its way out into the open with twists and turns even she hadn't seen coming.

She worked throughout the day and into the evening, the sun lowering across the room until she had to switch on the floor lamp angled overhead. Her work provided an escape and she was grateful. She'd spent more than enough time and energy on Kyle Brennan.

It was nearly ten o'clock before she realized she hadn't eaten. Not lunch, not dinner, not even so much as a snack. And while she would have preferred to keep going, the ever increasing protests rising up from her stomach were becoming harder and harder to ignore.

Betsy stood and wandered into the kitchen to examine the contents of her refrigerator. Last week's pizza was surely bad by now, as was the sub sandwich she hadn't finished before she left for New York. A glance at the clock brought a question mark to the notion of takeout just as her cell phone began to ring.

She flipped it open. "Hello?"

"So you made it back, safe and sound." Angela's voice, loud and boisterous, seeped through the phone and into her ear. "They kept tacking on so many days I was beginning to wonder if they were going to keep you there permanently."

"They wouldn't do that because then they wouldn't get their book." Leaning against the counter, Betsy gripped the edge with her free hand. "I didn't tell them about all the progress I was making in the hotel room each night."

"Good. I'd have been crushed if you hadn't come back."

She couldn't help but smile. With the unexpected kiss-off from Kyle still smarting, it was nice to know that someone, at least, felt so strongly about her. "I want to thank you for everything these past few weeks. You've been amazing."

"Tell me something I don't already know."

"You've been a great friend."

"Keep going."

"A terrific sounding board."

"Uh-huh."

"And a tremendous motivator."

"Oh?"

"Absolutely. I'm not sure I'd be this far along in my book without you. Your support and your enthusiasm, and most important, your friendship, has meant so much to me." And it was true. Angela Murphy was the one constant since she'd driven into Cedar Creek two weeks earlier. Well, Angela and Paxton Bridge, anyway.

"I—I don't know what to say."

A muffled thump in the background caught her by surprise. "What was that? Are you okay?"

"That—my dear friend, Betsy—was my darling husband...falling from his chair."

She gasped. "Is he okay?"

"Oh, he's fine. But you should see him right now. Boy, is he proud of himself."

"Why?"

"His theatrical reaction to my not knowing what to say."

"Ah." She wiped an apple on her shirt and then took

a bite, the crunch much louder than she intended. "Oh. Sorry about that. I kind of wrote through lunch."

"Lunch?"

"And dinner." Grabbing a napkin from the holder beside her potted violet, she wiped some juice from her chin. "By the way, thanks for watering the plants. They look great."

"Phew."

She laughed. "You were worried?"

"A little, yeah. I don't exactly have a green thumb. Mine tends to be kinda black. Like death."

"You did great."

"Hey, any chance you'd want to come over this weekend? I think it's time Tom and I reciprocated the barbecue thing. I'd like to ask Kyle and Callie but I can rethink that if you'd prefer."

Just the mention of Kyle's name made her shoulders droop.

Shaking her head free of a future that wasn't meant to be, she set her apple on the counter. "I really need to get some more writing done. After making them wait for so long for this book, I can't help but feel they might appreciate it being turned in early."

"Can you do that?"

"I think so. I've been on fire today. Getting away from—" She stopped, swallowed and started again. "Getting back to my own place will only speed the process."

"Getting back to your own place?" Angela sucked in her breath, the sound echoing through Betsy's ear. "Wait! Are you leaving?"

"I think it's best. I called Mr. Riley earlier today... told him I was going to head out sooner than previously anticipated. I told him he could keep the rent until he finds another tenant."

"But why?" Angela wailed. "I wanted you here while you wrote and then later, when you hit that post-book phase."

"Post-book phase?"

"Yeah. The part where you go to the movies and read books. I was hoping I could talk you into a shopping trip or a spa or something."

She closed her eyes against the longing to stay. Angela's idea sounded great, it really did. But knowing Kyle was next door, and that he wanted nothing to do with her, was simply more than she could take.

"Then come to New York when I finish. The shopping is *un*believable."

HE WAS FLIPPING THROUGH the channels when the call came, his partner's name popping up on the caller ID screen.

"Hey, Tom. What's up?"

"Incoming!"

Stretching his feet across the coffee table, he rolled his eyes upward. "Watching war movies again, partner?"

"Consider yourself warned."

"Warned? About wha—"

A pounding at his door cut him off midsentence.

"That," Tom said. "Good luck."

Confused, Kyle dropped the phone onto the couch and rose to his feet. When he reached the front door, he yanked it open to find Angela Murphy on the other side.

And if her tousled hair, wild eyes and slipper-clad feet were any indication, she was *mad*. At him.

He gulped. "Hey there, Ang...what brings you by at—" he glanced over his shoulder at the cable box "—eleven o'clock?"

"Stupid men," she hissed as she pushed her way past him and into his family room. "Stupid, stupid men."

"What'd Tom do now?"

She glared at him. "Tom's got nothing on you, buddy."

He puffed out his chest and inhaled sharply through his nose. "You're not telling me anything I don't already know."

Smacking him in the stomach with the backside of her hand, she leaned close, her eyes locked on his. "Give it a rest, Kyle."

"What? What'd I do?"

"For starters, you're stupid."

He snorted. "You covered that when I opened the door."

"Next, you're an idiot."

"Isn't that the same as being stupid?"

She glared at him again. "You're stupid for not seeing what's in front of your face. You're an idiot for letting it walk out of your life without a fight."

"She—she's leaving?" he whispered.

"You're darn straight she is. And it's all because of you. You and your Lila-created bitterness."

Slumping onto the couch, he brought his elbows to his thighs and his face into his hands. "When?"

"A few days."

"A few days," he repeated.

"Yeah...a few days. So what are you going to do about it?"

"What can I do?"

"Stop her!" Angela shouted.

Raising his eyes to meet hers, he swallowed, hard. "I've made a mess of things, you know that. I'm the last person who can stop her."

She dropped onto the sofa beside him. "Do you love her, Kyle?"

"Yes." The answer sounded so simple to his ears, felt so easy on his tongue.

"Then you're the *only* person who can stop her."

Chapter Twenty

She'd just passed the midway point of her manuscript when she heard it, a soft rustling sound outside her window. At first she chalked it up to nothing more than a squirrel or chipmunk, but when she heard voices, she froze.

Male voices. Deep, yet intentionally hushed.

Betsy quietly crept over to the window, some instinct warning her to stay out of sight. And then she saw them.

Two men, both wearing bandanas, crouched in the moonlit gap she and Kyle used as a pass-through. Unaware of her presence, the men pointed in the direction of the Brennan home, snatches of their conversation reaching her through the screen door.

"Hand me the lighter and get ready to run."

"Crap. I think I left it in my bike pouch."

"Get it."

She dropped to the ground as the bulkier of the two men stood and turned in her direction, her heart thumping in her chest. Had he seen her? After several long moments with no indication he had, she crawled her way into the kitchen. Pulling her cell phone from the counter where she'd left it, she dialed Kyle's number.

A woman answered.

Choking back the sob that threatened to make her words inaudible, Betsy pulled the phone tighter to her face. "My name is Betsy Anderson. I live next—"

"Hi, Betsy! It's Angela."

Caught between a mixture of relief and fear, she continued, her words shaky and hushed. "They're outside. In the hedge. I think they're going to set a fire."

She closed her eyes as she heard the phone being moved and Angela's muffled voice in the distance. Seconds later, Kyle's voice bellowed through her screen door as she sent up a silent prayer for his safety.

"Move and I'll shoot."

IT WAS SEVEN O'CLOCK the next morning before Kyle finally showed up, the adrenaline that surely got him through the night still evident on his face.

Steeling herself against the urge to throw herself into his arms, she simply pushed the screen door open and gestured him inside. "Is it over?"

Slowly he searched her face, nodding as he did. "We got 'em...thanks to you."

"All of them?"

"Yeah. It truly was a gang of thugs—four cousins hell-bent on teaching me a lesson for putting one of theirs in jail. But it's done now."

She felt her shoulders slump with relief. "And you're okay?"

"No. Not really."

Fear coursed through her body as she looked him over from top to bottom. "What happened? Did they hurt you?"

He reached out, touched her cheek with the backside

of his fingers. "Shh…." Pulling her into his arms, he held her close. "They didn't do a thing to me."

"But you said you're not okay."

"I'm not."

She wiggled her way out of his arms and stepped back. "I don't understand."

Raising his hands into the air, he brought them back down to cradle the back of his head. "Angela told me."

"Told you what?"

"That you're leaving for New York in a few days."

"Oh. That." She marched over to the computer table and sat down. "She's right. I am."

He dropped his hands to his sides and took a step forward, stopping almost as quickly. "But I thought you said you had another ten weeks or so."

She shrugged. "Things have changed."

"And by things you mean us?"

"I was deluding myself, Kyle. I thought we had something special here…something that was all ours." She allowed her gaze to flicker across the darkened screen. "But I was wrong. In your eyes I'll always be Lila."

He took a step closer. "I made a mistake."

"You make a lot of those." It was an honest assertion for which she had no guilt.

"You're right. But in this case I didn't see your note until it was too late. I thought you'd taken off for New York without so much as a look over your shoulder in my direction."

"And my calls the next evening?" she asked.

"By then the damage was done. I wasn't going to be an afterthought."

"You were my first thought, Kyle."

"I know that now. And I'm sorry." He closed the gap

between them, sinking to his knees when he reached her chair. "I'm sorry I didn't know. That I didn't have enough faith to know you wouldn't leave without telling me. But I was afraid for Callie. I didn't want her being hurt again."

"I wouldn't hurt Callie."

"I get that now. I think I knew it then, too. But fear has a way of chasing away facts. For you and for me."

She felt her resolve weakening.

"I can't live like this, Kyle. I can't live in the past anymore. Not mine and not yours." Holding her hand just out of his grasp she continued. "I understand that Lila hurt you. I get that. I also get that I've been through some mighty hard times myself. But I'm willing to consider that things can be different. I'm willing to love you with all my heart in spite of the very real possibility that you're going to be sent out on a call that might get you killed one day."

Her voice broke and she began to sob. The feel of his hands around her only made her sob harder.

"Please give me another chance, Betsy. Just one more. I promise you won't regret it." Lacing his hands through her hair he brought his lips to her ear. "Give me today. Please."

She shook her head as reality pushed aside the hope she felt brewing. "I need to write."

Hooking his index finger under her chin, he raised her head upward until their eyes met. "Didn't you tell me once that writing is what you do, not who you are?"

Tears streamed down her cheeks as she nodded her reply.

"Then put it aside for just this one day. Please, Betsy."

HE COULDN'T HELP IT. He loved looking at Betsy. Loved the way the sun sent shimmers of golden highlights through her otherwise soft brown mane. Loved the way her big brown eyes lit from within every time she saw something that captured her fancy—a family of squirrels, a rousing game of chipmunk tag, a squealing toddler on the nearby playground.

"Do you know how beautiful you are sitting there? Looking at the world like you're seeing it for the first time?" It was a thought that had struck him all afternoon as they lounged beside Paxton Lake. "I mean, I watch you and I see the way you soak up everything around you. And I guess I can't help but wonder where that comes from."

"I don't know what you mean."

"It's like the first time we met. You seemed truly interested in Paxton Bridge. Most people don't care."

She shrugged. "I think I was interested in you."

"You didn't come here for me."

"True. I simply saw a picture of the bridge and felt a pull. Since it was the first pull I'd felt in a year, I couldn't ignore it." She ducked her eyes from the path of the sun and flashed a smile in his direction. "I'm glad I didn't."

"You and me, both." Cocking his head toward the Paxton, he grinned. "Do you think it might be a wee bit strange to send a thank-you note to a bridge?"

"And you'd do that because..."

"It got you here." He shifted on the blanket, her flushed cheeks stirring a physical reaction he wasn't sure she was ready for yet. "I guess what I'm trying to say is that you seem to *see* where others only look."

"I'm not following."

"Take those squirrels earlier. You watched them for

a long time. I don't think they'd have even registered for most people." He scooted closer to her on the blanket, the remnants of their picnic lunch relegated to mere crumbs. "I like seeing things through your eyes. They seem far less tainted than mine."

The feel of her hands on his face caught him by surprise. Her words, even more so. "I think you just need to wear a different pair of glasses."

"Spoken like a writer," he quipped.

"No. Spoken like someone who cares very deeply for you."

Catching her hand in his, he turned it over and planted a kiss on her soft skin. "I believe that. I really do. And I think you're right about the glasses. In a way, at least."

She snuggled up inside his arms. "How so?"

"More than changing glasses, I think I just needed to get things in focus."

"And?" she asked.

"Lila was meant to be in my life. To give me Callie." Betsy's nod against his throat helped him continue, his thoughts streaming through his mouth with more clarity than he'd expected. "And you...you're in my life for an entirely different reason."

Reluctantly he released her from his arms so she could peer up at him. "And what's that?" she asked.

"To show me the meaning of true love."

With a gentle swipe of his thumbs, he cleared her face of the tears that fell, his own eyes burning from the truth. Never in his wildest imagination could he have ever foreseen meeting someone like Betsy—someone sweet and honest, loyal and caring, and so incredibly beautiful to boot.

"And on top of all that, I love the way you are with

Callie. It's as if you see her as a plus rather than a minus."

Betsy gasped. "A minus? How could anyone see Callie as a minus? She's smart and funny and talented and sweet and I consider it an honor to spend time with her." She bowed her head for a moment as she continued, her words difficult to hear. "It's why I wanted to leave early. The pain of losing both of you was more than I could handle."

Both...

Swallowing back the lump that threatened to render him speechless, he brushed his lips across her forehead. "You truly are a gift, Betsy Anderson—the most amazing gift I could ever imagine."

His heart squirmed under her seductive gaze only to be caught up short by the smile that exploded across her face. "She gets to come home now, doesn't she?"

"She?"

"Callie! Now that those guys are in jail, she gets to come home, right?"

He, too, smiled. "Day after tomorrow, yes."

"Why that long?" she asked.

"I'm working a long shift again tomorrow and school's out."

She sat up tall, her eyes glistening in the sun's rays. "I can watch her."

"You have to write, don't you?"

"While I'm writing she can color or do some writing of her own. After lunch I'll break for the day and we can do whatever we want."

He studied her closely, searching for any indication she was simply being polite, but there was none. Betsy truly loved his daughter. The knowledge made him swipe at a tear of his own as he pulled her close once again.

Suddenly, her tote bag vibrated against the blanket, the sound an unwelcome respite from a world that seemed to include no one else but the two of them.

Sitting up, she reached for her bag. "I'm sorry, but I should take this."

He listened as she talked, her cheerful greeting morphing into clipped statements.

"No. I absolutely can't come to New York tomorrow. I have a prior commitment."

Realizing the commitment she was referring to was Callie, he tried to wave her off but to no avail.

"Is there a reason they need me in person? Hmm, I didn't think so...I'll be available for a thirty-minute conference call at nine o'clock eastern time. Thanks, Hannah."

"You didn't have to do that," he said as she flipped the phone closed and stuffed it back inside her bag. "My mom could have watched her."

"I know that. But writing is what I do, not who I am. Remember?"

Reaching outward, he trailed a finger down her jaw, stopping it at her chin as he pulled her to within inches of his mouth. "I remember."

"Who I am is a woman in love with two people."

He stopped midway to her mouth. "Okay... Who is he?"

"Don't you mean, *she?*"

"She?" He repeated as his hand traveled around her neck only to stop and pull her the rest of the way, his mouth closing over hers as his tongue parted her lips. Their kiss, intense yet respectful, was the final reminder of what he knew to be true.

Betsy Anderson was a keeper.

Chapter Twenty-One

"Here, put these on."

She glanced down at the shorts he flung onto the bed along with a navy blue T-shirt that looked as if it was three sizes too big. "That's not my shirt. Mine's over there."

"I know. But yours leaves the top half of your back exposed."

"That didn't seem to bother you earlier today."

"True. But that's when the sun was shining and it was about twenty degrees warmer."

Clutching the sheets to her chest, she sat up in his bed, her tousled hair just one of many reminders of the way they'd spent the latter part of their day together. Time after time he'd entered her, their bodies moving together as one, each encounter surpassing the one before.

This was what she'd been searching for her whole life. Sure, writing was her dream...but finding true love was that and so much more.

"Where are we going?" she asked as she pulled his shirt over her head and struck a pose on his bed.

"Keep that up and we're not going anywhere."

"If that's supposed to be a threat, it's backfiring."

Grabbing his hand she pulled him down onto the sheets, making short work of the buttons he'd just painstakingly fastened. "I could stay here all night."

A frustrated moan emerged from his lips as he caught her fingers before they undid the final button. "My goal reaches a little further than that."

"Huh?" She closed her eyes as his lips brushed against hers.

"C'mon…finish up."

Opening her eyes, she followed him around the room as he pulled on the same pair of jeans she'd pulled off him not four hours earlier. "Should I be offended?"

He straightened up. "Offended?"

Scooting over to the edge of the bed, she wriggled into her shorts and zipped them up. "Here I am wanting to…well, you know…and all you want to do is get me out of here."

"Trust me, sweetheart, we'll be back."

She eyed him closely. "What are you up to?"

Feeling his hand close over hers, she couldn't help but smile, even as he tugged her to her feet and propelled her from his room. "No more questions."

"But I like questions," she protested.

He ushered her outside and over to his car. "I'll give you a hint."

"Okay…"

"We're going for a ride."

"I think I could have figured that out all on my own." She stepped back as he opened the door for her and guided her into the passenger seat, a smile teasing his lips. "How about another hint? One that's not quite so obvious this time?"

"Hmm. Well, I guess you could say it's official business."

"Official business?" she repeated. "We're going to the police department? Why?"

Bending slightly at the waist, he planted a kiss on her head before shutting the door and crossing to the driver's side. When he, too, was seated, he started the car and backed onto the road.

"It's not exactly that kind of official business."

"You're making my head hurt," she announced as she leaned back against the cloth interior. "How about I just sit over here and be quiet."

"Then I'd be sad."

"Why?"

"I'd miss the sound of your voice."

His honesty made her cheeks warm and her hands moisten. To think she'd nearly turned around en route to Cedar Creek out of embarrassment—embarrassment over searching for something that didn't exist.

But hope did exist.

It existed inside the human heart.

Sure, it had a tendency to get buried under life at times…but it was there, lurking, for anyone brave enough to seek it.

Hope had brought her back.

Love would keep it close.

The car slowed and she looked up, confusion narrowing her eyes. "What are we doing back here? Did you forget something?"

"Nope."

She studied him as he pulled the car to a stop in the exact same parking spot they'd filled earlier in the day. Without a word, he stepped from the car, his strong muscular form crossing to her side and offering her his hand.

"What's going on?" she asked as she, too, stepped from the car.

"Come with me. And you'll find out."

Motivated by curiosity and the sheer desire to spend every waking moment with this man, Betsy followed him down one moonlit path after another until they reached Paxton Bridge. With her hand firmly encased inside his, he pulled her onto the very top of the bridge.

"Kyle, I don't understand."

"After careful consideration I realized the thank-you note really wouldn't work."

"Thank you—" She stopped, an unexplainable joy rising up inside her being. "And so you decided to tell it in person?"

"No, not exactly." Dropping to one knee, Kyle took her left hand in his, his voice husky with emotion. "Since the Paxton is responsible for bringing us together, it seems only fitting it should be where we stand when we make it official."

"Official?" she whispered as a tear rolled down her face.

"Three weeks ago, I couldn't imagine sharing my life with another woman ever again. Now, I can't imagine living my life without you. Will you marry me, Betsy Anderson?"

Epilogue

"Are you ready?"

With a final glance in the floor-to-ceiling mirror Tom had propped against the tree for their use, Betsy nodded. "I've been ready since the moment he asked."

"Then let's do it," Angela said. Peering over Betsy's shoulder, she blew a kiss at herself. "You know what?"

"What's that?"

"You were right. I can stop traffic all on my own."

"I'm not too shabby for an old married lady."

Betsy smiled at the reflection of her friend. "Are you kidding? You'd stop traffic, married or not."

Angela smiled. "Well, in about six months, Tom and I will have a little traffic-stopper of our own."

"You're pregnant?"

"Yep."

Squealing, Betsy turned from the mirror and wrapped her arms around her friend. "How long have you known?"

"I couldn't figure out why I was feeling so tired all the time. And then one night it hit me."

She peeked through the line of oak trees that separated them from the bridge, her eyes searching for Kyle's best man. "Is he ecstatic?"

"Well, I've gotten a foot rub every night for the past week along with a box of chocolate and a bouquet of flowers, too."

"Flowers and chocolate every day?" she asked as she pulled her focus from the crowd of people who'd assembled by the foot of the bridge—a crowd that included most of the Cedar Creek Police Department, as well as her agent and editor and a photographer from *Dreams Come True Magazine*.

"Every day. Like clockwork."

"I'm glad. You deserve it." Glancing into the mirror one last time, she inhaled deeply, the setting sun warm against her face. "Angela?"

"Yes?"

"I've never been this happy in my entire life."

"And this is just the beginning. It's only going to get better from here on out."

Stretching her hand outward, she grasped her friend's hand inside her own. "Thank you, Angela. For everything."

"You're welcome. Now let's get out of here before my little traffic-stopper sends me off in search of a porta-potty."

"Roger that." Squaring her shoulders, she inhaled deeply once again, willing her mind to remember every detail of this day. Every detail of Kyle's face when he saw her, every word they exchanged in the presence of their friends and family.

She looked toward the keyboardist for her cue as Angela headed down the pathway that would lead her to the bridge. When her friend had reached her final destination, the music started, signaling the start of a life she couldn't wait to embrace.

Step by step she walked down the path, the faces of their guests blurring in her memory as she rounded the corner toward Paxton Bridge. As she began her ascent onto the stone structure that had started it all, their eyes met—hers, Kyle's and Callie's.

And while the official proclamation was still moments away, she already knew it to be true…

They were a family. Forever and always.

* * * * *

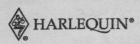

COMING NEXT MONTH

Available August 10, 2010

#1317 BABY BOMBSHELL
Babies & Bachelors USA
Lisa Ruff

#1318 DUSTY: WILD COWBOY
The Codys: The First Family of Rodeo
Cathy McDavid

#1319 THE MOMMY PROPOSAL
The Lone Star Dads Club
Cathy Gillen Thacker

#1320 HIS HIRED BABY
Safe Harbor Medical
Jacqueline Diamond

HARCNM0710

REQUEST YOUR FREE BOOKS!
2 FREE NOVELS PLUS 2 FREE GIFTS!

HARLEQUIN®

American ★ Romance®

Love, Home & Happiness!

YES! Please send me 2 FREE Harlequin® American Romance® novels and my 2 FREE gifts (gifts are worth about $10). After receiving them, if I don't wish to receive any more books, I can return the shipping statement marked "cancel." If I don't cancel, I will receive 4 brand-new novels every month and be billed just $4.24 per book in the U.S. or $4.99 per book in Canada. That's a saving of at least 15% off the cover price! It's quite a bargain! Shipping and handling is just 50¢ per book.* I understand that accepting the 2 free books and gifts places me under no obligation to buy anything. I can always return a shipment and cancel at any time. Even if I never buy another book from Harlequin, the two free books and gifts are mine to keep forever.

154/354 HDN E5LG

Name _____ (PLEASE PRINT)

Address _____ Apt. #

City _____ State/Prov. _____ Zip/Postal Code

Signature (if under 18, a parent or guardian must sign)

Mail to the **Harlequin Reader Service:**
IN U.S.A.: P.O. Box 1867, Buffalo, NY 14240-1867
IN CANADA: P.O. Box 609, Fort Erie, Ontario L2A 5X3

Not valid for current subscribers to Harlequin® American Romance® books.

Want to try two free books from another line?
Call 1-800-873-8635 or visit www.morefreebooks.com.

* Terms and prices subject to change without notice. Prices do not include applicable taxes. N.Y. residents add applicable sales tax. Canadian residents will be charged applicable provincial taxes and GST. Offer not valid in Quebec. This offer is limited to one order per household. All orders subject to approval. Credit or debit balances in a customer's account(s) may be offset by any other outstanding balance owed by or to the customer. Please allow 4 to 6 weeks for delivery. Offer available while quantities last.

Your Privacy: Harlequin is committed to protecting your privacy. Our Privacy Policy is available online at www.eHarlequin.com or upon request from the Reader Service. From time to time we make our lists of customers available to reputable third parties who may have a product or service of interest to you. If you would prefer we not share your name and address, please check here. ☐

Help us get it right—We strive for accurate, respectful and relevant communications. To clarify or modify your communication preferences, visit us at www.ReaderService.com/consumerschoice.

HAR10R

HARLEQUIN®

A *Romance*

FOR EVERY MOOD™

Spotlight on

─ Heart & Home ─

Heartwarming romances
where love can happen
right when you least expect it.

See the next page to enjoy a sneak peek
from Harlequin® American Romance®,
a Heart and Home series.

*Five hunky Texas single fathers—five stories from
Cathy Gillen Thacker's* LONE STAR DADS *miniseries.
Here's an excerpt from the latest,* THE MOMMY PROPOSAL
from Harlequin American Romance.

"I hear you work miracles," Nate Hutchinson drawled.
Brooke Mitchell had just stepped into his lavishly appointed
office in downtown Fort Worth, Texas.

"Sometimes, I do." Brooke smiled and took the sexy
financier's hand in hers, shook it briefly.

"Good." Nate looked her straight in the eye. "Because
I'm in need of a home makeover—fast. The son of an old
friend is coming to live with me."

She was still tingling from the feel of his warm palm.
"Temporarily or permanently?"

"If all goes according to plan, I'll adopt Landry by
summer's end."

Brooke had heard the founder of Nate Hutchinson
Financial Services was eligible, wealthy and generous to a
fault. She hadn't known he was in the market for a family,
but she supposed she shouldn't be surprised. But Brooke
had figured a man as successful and handsome as Nate
would want one the old-fashioned way. *Not that this was
any of her business...*

"So what's the child like?" she asked crisply, trying not
to think how the marine-blue of Nate's dress shirt deepened
the hue of his eyes.

"I don't know." Nate took a seat behind his massive
antique mahogany desk. He relaxed against the smooth
leather of the chair. "I've never met him."

"Yet you've invited this kid to live with you permanently?"

"It's complicated. But I'm sure it's going to be fine."

Obviously Nate Hutchinson knew as little about teenage

HAREXP0810

boys as he did about decorating. But that wasn't her problem. Finding a way to do the assignment without getting the least bit emotionally involved was.

Find out how a young boy brings Nate and Brooke together in THE MOMMY PROPOSAL, coming August 2010 from Harlequin American Romance.

HARLEQUIN®

Super Romance®

Fan favourite

Molly O'Keefe

brings readers a brand-new miniseries

the NOTORIOUS O'NEILLS

Beginning with

The Temptation of Savannah O'Neill

Escaping her family's reputation was all
Savannah O'Neill ever wanted. Then Matt Woods
shows up posing as a simple handyman, and she
can see there's much more to him than meets the
eye. However tempted to get beneath his surface,
she knows that uncovering his secrets could expose
her own. But as Matt begins to open himself up to
Savannah, that's when the trouble really begins....

Available August 2010 wherever books are sold.